UNLOCHED

CANDICE LEMON-SCOTT

ODYSSEY
BOOKS

Published by Odyssey Books in 2012

978-0-9872325-7-1

www.odysseybooks.com.au

National Library of Australia
Cataloguing-in-Publication entry

Author: Lemon-Scott, Candice
Title: Unloched / Candice Lemon-Scott
ISBN: 9780987232571 (pbk.)
9780987232588 (ebook)
Dewey Number: A823.4

Cover design and typesetting by Odyssey Books
Cover image by Igor Balasanov via iStockPhoto

For my husband Neil, whose support along my writing journey has been unwavering.

1

Lauren stood by the bed. She noticed that her mother's skin, once brown and wrinkled from hours spent in her garden, had paled and shrivelled. Her arms and legs were stick-like, jutting out from the edges of her thinning flannel night-gown. Her round stomach sat heavily over her hips. Lauren bent down to kiss her mother's dry cheek. Gisella's lips puckered the air. Her smell was stale, not like the fresh air aroma she once carried. The scent of dirt and fresh green grass was gone, replaced with one that Lauren couldn't quite grasp. It was a worn-out type of smell, of waiting too long. Like someone at the airport, between flights.

'Still cold outside?' her mother asked.

'It was foggy this morning. I think it'll be a nice afternoon though. You should get out for some fresh air. Do the nurses do that?'

'Do what?'

'Take you out?'

'For what?'

'A walk, Mother. Do the nurses take you out for a walk each day?'

'Can't afford to get sick.'

'They should.'

'Should what?'

'Take you out for a walk.'

'Can't afford to get sick.'

'Okay Mum, have it your way.'

'What do you mean by that?'

'Nothing, I just thought a walk would be nice for you. You used to love the outdoors.'

'What walk?'

Lauren didn't respond, instead busying herself with straightening up the room. Not that there was much to straighten. A pillow plumped. A spare blanket folded. A newspaper closed. Lauren allowed herself to momentarily wonder how much of her mother's vagueness was from the drugs she was given, and how much was a deliberate attempt at avoidance. Suddenly she needed to pee.

'Okay to use your bathroom Mum?'

'It's not mine.'

Lauren took her response as a yes. She moved to the ensuite, locking the wide door, though there was no need to. Her mother could no longer even get out of bed without assistance. She leant her hand on the cold silver bar beside the toilet. Everything within the white-washed bathroom was a reminder of her mother's ineptitude at doing anything for herself any more. She blew her nose, peed, and washed her hands. Her pale skin, and wrinkles that had just begun to form on her brow in the last few months, stood out against the glaring fluorescent light. *I should start wearing makeup*, she thought.

'It stinks of antiseptic in there. I should bring in some aromatherapy oils to burn. They're very calming.'

'Make me sneeze, that's what they'd do.'

Lauren sat in the bucket chair beside her mother. She felt too low next to the raised bed, but standing was no good either. She flipped through the newspaper she'd just closed.

'God, it's like reading a tabloid these days. Where's the real news?'

'Too depressing. No one wants to hear it.'

'I s'pose.'

She put the newspaper back on the side table and felt a cold hand descend on her warm one. Lauren stared at her mother's hand on top of her own. The paper-thin skin that covered her veins looked like it might break with the slightest movement. So Lauren held still, her back bent over the chair uncomfortably, while her mother spoke in a raspy, thin voice.

'There's something I want you to do for me, Lauren.'

'What Mother?' Lauren said.

'The houseboat. I want you to sell it for me.'

Lauren fought the urge to pull away from her mother and storm out, leaving her to fend for herself. *Paper-thin hands.* She reminded herself that her mother had always done what she thought was best. Words she said to herself almost every day. Lauren remained held by her mother's weak hands.

'Why, Mother?'

'No need for it anymore.'

'Yes, but why now?'

'Good a time as any.'

'But it's been years. Decades.'

Lauren heard her mother's breathing quicken as she tried to sit up. She leaned over, her sour breath close.

'Decade. Not decades. Don't be so melodramatic. It needs to be sold. That's all.'

Her mother's hand felt heavier on hers now. Lauren looked uncomfortable as she leaned sideways across the bed. She knew her mother couldn't be stressed in any way.

'I'll put in an ad tomorrow,' Lauren said.

'No!'

Lauren felt her mother's hand begin to tremble.

'I need you to fix it up first. Clean it up. Make it nice. So you'd want to buy it yourself. Like it used to be. You remember how it used to be, don't you?'

'Of course I remember. How could I forget?'

Her mother ignored the implication. They didn't talk about the past.

'Then you'll go? Tomorrow?'

This time Lauren did pull away. But gently. *Paper-thin hands.* She sat in the chair opposite and stared out the window, stained with dirty raindrops. She crossed her arms, trying to block out the memories, not wanting to remember. She hadn't thought of her sister for months. She had managed to block her out almost entirely now, so she didn't see Trina in the mirror anymore. And it had taken a long time. At first she remembered only their similarities. The same ski-jump nose, the same dimple in their chins, the same wispy ash-blonde hair. But then she managed to focus on their differences. The mole on Trina's left ear. Long nails compared to her bitten ones. The front tooth that had been chipped the time Trina crashed into another child at a party. And then, finally, she didn't think about her at all. In the mirror was only Lauren.

'Lauren. *Lauren.*'

She turned back to her mother.

'It's time to get rid of what's passed. I need you to help me.'

Lauren answered by lifting herself from the chair.

'Look at that nightgown. It's had it. I'll be in tomorrow. I'll bring you a new one. Size 10? We'll talk more then. Okay?'

Lauren kissed her mother on the forehead before she could reply.

2

Trina loaded her leather overnight bag and toiletry case into the boot of the Saab. Graham struggled down the stairs with everything else. He dropped the luggage and looked disapprovingly at the way Trina had arranged her bags. He removed her belongings and proceeded to re-arrange the boot, squeezing in each item like they were pieces of a jigsaw.

'Right. We're all set,' he said, clapping his hands in satisfaction. 'Heater off? Lights out?'

'I'll double check.'

Trina ran up the stairs. *Heater's off.* She quickly scoured the upstairs rooms. They were all dim, with just the muted rays of sunlight filtering in. *Lights are off.* She pulled the edge of the doona, straightening out a narrow crease that ran from corner to corner. Back downstairs she flitted in and out of rooms to ensure nothing was amiss. She checked that the answering machine was on. The red light flashed three times, paused, and flashed three times again. The rhythmical blinking was like a lighthouse, its fluorescent beacon a warning to stay away. But somehow Trina had been continuously drawn to it. Over the past two days she had replayed those messages so many times she knew the words by heart. This time she did not press play. Instead, she held the stop/pause button until the light became constant. The words erased.

Trina opened the Saab's passenger side door and climbed in. She reached across the centre console and kissed her husband. She felt his lips, warm against hers, and knew he sensed her fear.

'Thanks,' she said.

'What for?'

'I don't think I could do it on my own.'

'You sure you want to do this?'

Trina had never been so *unsure* of anything in her life. It had taken her years to remove herself completely from the rest of her family. She'd moved to the other side of the city, established a life that didn't leave much room for visitations, and formed a relationship with Graham, so that she need never feel lonely and want to go back. Though she visited her mother twice a year and spoke to her on the telephone, it was always superficial talk about gardens and work, and Trina liked it that way. At first her mother had spoken to her about Lauren. She had told Trina that the two of them should 'patch things up'—as though it were as simple as sprinkling lawn seed in the front yard and waiting for it to grow, filling in the bare patches of earth. But eventually she had stopped mentioning Lauren and things had been easy after that.

Until now. Until her mother's messages, pleading with her to go back. Trina was not sure she wanted to do this. In fact, she was entirely sure she didn't want to do this. She was still unable to explain it to herself. Perhaps she felt guilty, or just plain tired. Maybe her mother's nagging had finally worn her down.

If Trina had been willing to be honest with herself, her decision may have been different. She might have been able to admit that she was doing this because, despite everything her mother had done to her, she still wanted her approval. She still wanted to hear her mother tell her she was proud of her. Instead Trina answered her husband as well as her conscious thoughts would allow, though the slight tremble in her voice and the tightness in her chest betrayed her.

'I'm sure I want to do this, Graham. It's something I need to do.'

'For your mother?'

'For me.'

Graham nodded, but Trina could see he didn't understand that parents weren't always on your side.

3

Lauren pushed aside the houseboat's chocolate and fawn curtains. Even now she was certain the thin, squiggly lines formed the shape of chicks. Their heads stretched forward as though in search of the light. When she was a child, her mother had insisted in a bored tone that it was just a pattern. She said there were no chickens. Not even when the curtains were pulled taut across the small window. She said if they were meant to be chicks they would have made the curtains yellow. One time Lauren had instructed her mother that some baby chicks were brown. Her mother had slapped her across the face in response, yet Lauren recalled that Trina had been the one to hold her hand to her cheek for the rest of the afternoon. They had been like that as children; one would often feel the other's pain and it somehow made the blows seem more bearable.

Lauren wound the stiff plastic handle on the window round and round. The rusted chain lengthened and stretched. She pressed her nose against the fly screen, breathing in the fresh outside air. She opened the rest of the windows until the all-too-familiar smell of mildew had disappeared.

With the curtains open, Lauren could see more clearly.

She glanced around at the miniature lounge, bedroom and kitchen. Her gaze held on the tiny sink. The white plastic plug was still attached to a thin chain, as though it were a precious commodity that would be irreplaceable if lost. It reminded her of the pens attached to the benches at the bank. It always annoyed her that the chain of tiny silver balls prevented her from lifting the pen high or using it at the other end of the bench, where it wouldn't reach. The plug had the same effect. She was never able to have the satisfaction of ripping the plug from the sink when the dishes were finally done. Instead, she could only push it aside.

She finally moved her eyes away from the sink. It amazed her how the boat still looked exactly the same as she remembered, though she hadn't seen it in almost ten years. What stunned Lauren more was the familiarity of every handle, every ripple in the linoleum, and the feeling of being suffocated that returned to her now. It made her feel as though she was a teenager again, where her life between summer holidays on the boat and now had existed only in a dream. Her head became light and her stomach churned as the thin walls shifted around her. Lauren swung the door open and stepped onto the splintered wooden deck. She bent forward, her neck craning over the edge like the chickens on the curtains. Her vomit splashed into the water and dispersed. Seagulls swarmed and fed.

'Scavengers!' Lauren cried out across the empty lake.

4

Trina grasped her husband's arm.

'Pull over,' she groaned.

Graham glanced over at Trina, frowning.

'Pull over,' she repeated, squeezing his arm tighter.

Her manicured nails dug into his flesh and Graham winced before switching on the indicator. He slowed the Saab to a stop, skidding along the gravel. Trina wrenched open the passenger side door and threw up on the ground.

'You want some water?' Graham asked, pushing a bottle towards her.

Trina waved him away, her hand flapping up and down behind her.

'Must have been that burger. Best to steer clear of chicken at roadhouses. Never know how long the food's been sitting there,' Graham said, trying to be consoling.

Trina doubled over again.

'Sorry, guess I shouldn't be saying that right now.'

'Just get me a towel.'

Graham hurried to the back of the car. He unzipped his bag, pulling out shirts and trousers before finding a cream bathsheet.

'Here!'

Trina snatched the towel and wiped her mouth and her chin. 'I'm alright now.'

Graham pulled back onto the highway. Trina leant her head against the cold, tinted window.

They travelled the rest of the way with few words spoken. As they passed through Rosedale and took the turn-off to Loch Sport, the landscape became flat and lifeless. Dusk brought with it the type of stillness Trina constantly fought off with business appointments, late lunches with friends and the frantic cleaning of her impeccable home. Here she could only be held and forced to be part of the moment. She tried to shift in her seat but remained uncomfortable. She wished she was driving, but knew that would also bring little distraction as the road stretched on and on until she began to wonder if the road led anywhere, or just kept going.

Kangaroos dotted the landscape; black silhouettes against a washed out orange sky. Clouds hung in the air as though suspended on a scrim at the back of the universe's stage. Fog was dropped in, blurring the edges as Trina stared out the window. As they neared the township, she could recall the soft bends in the road before they appeared, and yet she didn't remember much about leaving Loch Sport after that last summer, before her final year at high school. All she remembered was sitting in the back of her mother's beat up old station wagon with the sense of drifting away, becoming enveloped in the fog.

5

Christmas in the palliative care unit had been unbearable, with its tokenistic tinsel and two-foot plastic pine tree in the corner of the day room. But there was no birth to celebrate, only death surrounding Gisella, with its smell of antiseptic, reminding her she was next. Only the next never came. Christmas came. The day of reflection, of idle chitchat about holidays, and Uncle Bob's fishing trip after they had to row him back in to shore when he got stranded on a sand bank. It was the day of memories. All Gisella needed was more memories.

She picked up the remote, pressed the wide green button and watched the annual re-run of *Miracle on 34th Street*. She drowned out her orchestra of memories with myths about Santa and bratty children declaring their parents liars.

The credits were rolling, and her half-eaten lunch had been taken away, when Lauren arrived with her arms full as usual, a shiny red package held firmly against her chest.

'Merry Christmas.'

'Is it?' Gisella replied curtly.

The shiny red package landed on her crisp white sheet, leaning heavily against Gisella's belly button.

'I got you a little something. Hope you like it.'

Lauren began tearing off pieces of sticky tape and Gisella wondered why she had bothered to wrap the damn thing in the first place. Perhaps to prove how incapable she was of doing anything for herself anymore.

'It's a jewellery box,' Lauren announced, as if Gisella couldn't see that for herself. 'I thought it would be better than shoving your jewellery into one of your side table drawers. It's got compartments for rings and bracelets. And look. You can hang your necklaces here. See?'

'Thanks. I didn't get anything for you. Bit hard in here. I can't exactly go out gift shopping. Unless you'd like me to get some flowers delivered to the room? I think we can do that. Of course, it's usually the other way around. I mean the visitor's usually the one giving the patient the flowers.'

'No, that's fine. I didn't expect you to…'

The jewellery box started bouncing around on Gisella's stomach as thick raspy coughs wracked her body.

'God, Mum.'

Gisella tried to breathe as Lauren shuffled pillows and tried to pull her mother into a more upright position. Finally her breathing returned to normal and Lauren pressed a glass of water into her hand. She took it shakily. Lauren had become a better nurse to her over the years than the young things that flitted in and out of her room.

'Don't try to talk too much Mum, okay?'

'Don't take that away from me too. I haven't spoken two words all day,' she snapped.

'Just don't exert yourself.'

'Don't concern yourself. I'm not about to go for a jog.'

'Did they give you anything special for lunch?'

'Oh, not really. Same old. You know how it is. A mushy pile of indistinguishable vegetables. A slab of meat. All tastes the same, you know.'

The new young nurse came into the room, her uniform was as impeccable as always. The only difference to her usual straight-laced, not-a-hair-out-of-place look were plastic red and white striped candy canes dangling from her ears. She looked at her watch and scribbled on the notepad at the end of her bed. Gisella guessed she couldn't be much older than twenty. She came up alongside Gisella and began taking her blood pressure.

'We're not telling fibs now are we?' she said, smoothing her hand over her tightly knotted brown bun.

'Wouldn't dream of it.'

She smiled with her red mouth at Lauren, and Gisella could have hit her, if she'd had the energy.

'We had a very special lunch today. Turkey roast with apple sauce and a mince tart for dessert. Didn't we?'

'You eat this mush too, do you?' Gisella replied.

'I didn't have lunch here. I'm on the afternoon shift.' She whispered to Lauren as though Gisella couldn't hear her, 'Had lunch with the relos.'

The nurse failed to pick up on the sarcasm. *No sense of humour either.* Without so much as a smile for her patient, she scribbled on the pad again and left. Gisella tried to picture the nurse sitting around with her family. She could imagine her soft voice being drowned out by a gaggle of nieces and nephews under the age of ten and a raucous father laughing at the head of the table. It was the type of family she had never been part of. It had always been Christmas on the houseboat with just her and the girls. With her always on the outer, and them in quiet communication she could never decipher.

'I brought you some new magazines. *Reader's Digest*, *Woman's Day*. They'd sold out of *New Idea*. Did you see *The Bold and the Beautiful* yesterday, Mum?'

'Yes, that Brooke gets my goat. She's cracking onto Ridge yet again. Why won't she take the hint?'

'I missed it. I was too busy in the garden.'

'You haven't killed all my plants, I hope?'

'No, they're fine Mum.'

'What about the roses? You have to prune them back.'

'I know, Mum. I will. Don't worry.'

Gisella knew that Lauren was no green thumb. Her plants were probably all wilted and dying now summer was coming on, if they weren't dead already. But there was no use complaining. It's not like she would ever see her garden again. Still, it bothered her to think of it gone. Even after she was.

Conversation ran out quickly and Gisella switched on the TV to fill the quiet. They watched Jerry Springer together. Two obese women dressed in fluorescent bikinis, baring their tattoos on breasts and butts, were wrestling each other over a thin, moustached man. Their breasts hung over his face.

'You'd think one that size would be enough for him,' Gisella said.

'Horrid!' Lauren commented.

They both watched on, Gisella enjoying being disgusted by the staged rivalry. When it was finished, Lauren raised herself from the chair, brushed down her skirt and kissed her on the cheek.

'See you on Monday, Mum.'

'Got a big date planned, have you? Now that your annoying old mother is out of your hair? Well, don't let me keep him waiting.'

As soon as the words were spoken she wondered why she'd said them. Lauren hadn't been with a man for years. Sometimes she blamed herself. She knew having to care for her ill mother hadn't been easy. But nor did she see Lauren longing for anyone. Not for company. Certainly not for sex. She guessed she could understand that with what happened. *Still, she should have gotten over it, like I got over Christian*, she thought. *That was life.* Then again, perhaps she was wrong. Perhaps she could never understand.

'No, it's nothing like that Mum. I can stay a bit longer, if you like?'

'Don't worry about me. Oh, Trina's here.'

Gisella noticed Lauren stiffen as her sister entered the room. *So sad, the two of them.* She had hoped that somehow Christmas would sort things out. Weren't people supposed to get sentimental and forget old grievances in these times? Even now, neither daughter wanted to resolve things, and Gisella felt like screaming at them both to grow up. But she didn't have any energy left for conflicts. Instead she watched them nod acknowledgement in a polite attempt to keep their mother from seeing their hate. They didn't understand that mothers don't need to see these things. They feel them.

Gisella said nothing as Lauren slipped by her sister, her gait faster on the way out than it had been on the way in. Trina took Lauren's place at the bedside with her hairy husband. The way he swung his arms about as he carried his heavy frame and the way he wore that ridiculous beard reminded Gisella of a gorilla.

'Hi Mum,' Trina said, holding onto her husband's arm as though she'd fall over if she let go.

'Trina! Nice of you to drop by today.'

'Merry Christmas. Sorry I couldn't get here earlier. Shocking traffic. We have to be over at Graham's parents by three, so I don't have long.'

'Sorry to cause you so much inconvenience,' Gisella said sarcastically.

'I didn't mean it like that Mum... The nurse seems in good spirits today, having to work Christmas Day and all.'

'Pity she wasn't when she took my blood pressure earlier. I thought my arm was going to fall off, she squeezed the damn thing so tight.'

'How is it in here? Okay? They treat you well?'

'Well enough,' she replied, knowing Trina didn't really care or want to know what it was like, dying in a small room with people who saw you only as part of a job that had to be done.

They sat in silence for a few minutes, Gisella knowing no truth was about to be spoken, which left little else. She sat quiet in her thoughts as Trina and her husband glanced around the room, as though the blank walls and pale blue curtains were fascinating. She was tempted to tell them they weren't in an art gallery, but kept her mouth shut. Trina's visits, though one-dimensional, were too rare to warrant beginning an argument. Trina shifted her gaze to the jewellery box and finally Gisella saw an opening for conversation.

'Lauren brought me this.'

'Oh?' Trina said before hastily changing the subject. 'You've been reading *Woman's Day* I see. Anything interesting?'

Trina picked up the magazine and flipped through it as though looking for a scripted conversation she could have. Gisella doubted Trina read cheap gossip magazines. She probably bought *Vogue* or some other fashion magazine. One with anorexic models dressed in see-through sequined blouses on the cover and advertising $500 scarves that wouldn't keep a ferret warm.

'I haven't read it yet. Lauren dropped it around before.'

'Right.'

Afternoon tea came. Gisella ate even though she didn't feel hungry. Trina glanced at her watch and fidgeted. Her husband took over the conversation and once he did Gisella wished he'd shut up and leave her in peace.

'Did you hear about the floods out west? Terrible,' he said.

'Yes, terrible,' she said through gritted teeth.

'Global warming,' he said.

'Hmmm?' Gisella, raising an eyebrow in mock interest.

'Global warming,' he repeated.

'Yes, yes. I might be dying but I can still hear,' Gisella said tartly.

'Mum,' Trina interjected.

'All I meant was, what of it?'

'Well, these extreme weather conditions we're getting. Drought. Flood. It's a symptom wouldn't you say?'

'A symptom? No… Are you familiar with Henry Lawson, Greg?'

'It's Graham,' Trina said. 'Of course he knows who Lawson is.'

Fool can't even speak for himself.

'His poetry. Read it. If you read, that is. Always been that way in this grand but harsh country of ours.'

'Not like this. Have you seen the stats?'

'That Gore character? He has a lot to answer for.'

'That's scientific evidence.'

'Science, piance. Rubbish! Those scientists want to keep themselves in a job. Gotta come up with something to say. A reason to exist.'

Gisella noticed Trina's hand tensely placed on her husband's forearm. He backed down.

'Maybe you're right. Who's to say?'

No balls on that one.

'Who's to say?' Gisella agreed, satisfied.

That night Gisella lay back against her bed, shifting the thick pillows down again. She looked at the magazines, jewellery box and pieces of torn wrapping paper covering her side table. She gazed across the room. Nothing had changed. Not that she expected Christmas to magically transform her view, not in any real way. After all she was a practical woman. She could still smell the alcohol on Trina's breath as she had kissed her goodbye, reminding her that her daughter still had a life while her own was slipping away. 'See you soon, okay Mum?' she had said. 'Soon?' *Ha*. She knew that would be the last time she'd see her daughter. She didn't believe in miracles, or magic, or any of that paranormal nonsense. Then again, you never knew for certain. She closed her eyes, allowing the day to drift over her body.

6

Unpacking and cleaning could wait. Lauren needed food. She sifted through her basket and pulled out a can of spaghetti in cheesy tomato sauce and a loaf of bread that was now indented along one side. She reached up to the overhead cupboard and found a pan, still in the same place as she remembered. She lit the stovetop, the gas slowly breathing life into the boat as tiny yellow sparks turned into flame. Lauren didn't realise just how much she had been in need of food until the aroma of tomato sauce filled her nostrils. She took the spaghetti off the stove a little too early but downed the lukewarm meal in a few large spoonfuls.

After lunch Lauren was able to think more clearly. But with that came the realisation that she was alone. The water lapping against the edge of the boat seemed deafening against the quiet inside. She decided to go for a quick swim before getting started on the houseboat. She pulled on a pair of navy blue one-piece bathers, stepped down onto the pontoon and dove deeply into the cool water. Ever since she was a child, swimming had brought her a sense of calmness and clarity. It was the only time her body felt light and free as she concentrated on the even strokes of freestyle. *Push. Inhale. Push.*

Exhale. Inhale. Exhale. Inhale. Exhale. She made her way out to the centre of the lake, the water darkening beneath her. She felt the increasing resistance as small ripples formed in the deeper water. She pushed harder through it, feeling her shoulder and leg muscles coming alive as she propelled herself forward. She began breathing hard and tumbled beneath the water to head back towards the miniaturised houseboat. She smiled at the doll's house appearance it had from such a distance and took another breath before heading back towards reality.

Lauren remembered the first time she had swum away from the security and confinement of the houseboat. She had been only four years old at the time. It was a cool day for summer, with a light breeze chilling the air slightly. She had pleaded with her mother to take her in the water. After much coaxing she had finally agreed. She watched from the pontoon as her mother slid into the water. She disappeared for a second before her head bobbed back up on the surface. Her mother stretched her arms up towards her and suddenly the water seemed much further away from her than it had before. She began shifting her feet away from the edge of the pontoon, curling her toes as though they brought her a safer distance from the water. Her mother tried to reassure her that it was okay, but even though she was usually right about these things Lauren's mind was already racing— telling herself she couldn't do it. She heard her mother's *I'm getting annoyed at you* tone, but she was already heading in the other direction and she somehow couldn't turn back. The more the pitch of her mother's voice rose, the more agitated she became.

Before she knew it her father had picked her up in his big arms and jumped high in the air and into the water with her. Her head went under the water for a second and everything became muffled. The sound of her mother was no longer loud and high but a fuzzy buzzing sound, like a bee. When her head and shoulders broke the surface of the water, big fat drops filled her open mouth as she shrieked with the fun of it all. Her dad proceeded to swish her around in the water and she couldn't help giggling as he twisted her this way and that, making snake tracks along the surface.

Lauren was having so much fun that she didn't notice her mother's face had turned pinkish and squished up into an angry ball. But she did notice her mother screech at her father that he was an idiot for playing that way. The words went on and on and she was soon being reluctantly dragged back to the edge of the pontoon. Her teeth chattered from the cold as her mother wrapped a large towel around her so tightly she almost couldn't breathe. Soon she was as warm and dry as Trina, who sat obliviously on the decking playing with a pile of sand and spade.

7

It wasn't until after Christmas that Gisella realised she wasn't going to die and discovered that her thin breath would continue to keep her alive. In the beginning she thought she had just been holding out for Christmas. But the day had come and gone; it seemed post Christmas passings were reserved for people whose families celebrated together. For families who sat around eating roast and pudding until they had to loosen their belts. For families who sat around a lit pine tree, passing each other green parcels via an excited child in a red hat. It was then she knew God must have further plans for her.

Gisella briefly questioned why she had not found the houseboat's purpose sooner. Then she realised it had not been the right time, until now. She remembered a bittersweet contentment as she had forged her plan. It seemed almost laughable to her that the boat would be given renewed life when she was waiting for the end of her own.

She had idled away the long hours contemplating her impending death. And finally it had come to her. She had something left to do, and God wasn't going to let her go until she'd done it. The houseboat needed a purpose. And it was she who had to give it one. Only then would she be able to slip across to the other side, knowing she had done all she could. The houseboat had been the one thing that had pushed her daughters apart and it was the one thing that would bring them back together. It was her duty to do this for Lauren and Trina. Her family. Her real family. She would reunite two halves, who at one time decided they could go it alone. She imagined herself smiling down from heaven at her children as they shared good times and good conversation. She could see them looking over childhood photographs, remembering the good times with their mother. She liked the way photos did that—captured the happy moments, as though that was all that ever existed. They'd pore over photos of their mother putting the final touches on a sandcastle. Of them running away from the surf as it crashed down at their feet. Of a lazy afternoon sitting on the decking with Lauren bouncing on her knee while Trina took an unfocused shot of them both. Yes, that's what they'd remember. The good things. They'd smile with the fondness of memories, until they remembered their mother was no longer there to share the joy. Then there'd be a few tears shed out of grief, but renewed happiness that they had found one another. Smiles through the tears. Light out of darkness. Wakefulness from sleep.

8

The lights of the houses were dull, as though they weren't quite ready to accept that night was falling. Dark clouds hung just above the horizon, allowing a sliver of muted light to fight the oncoming darkness.

'Looks like it's going to rain tomorrow,' Graham said. 'Hope the roof's okay on the houseboat.'

'I'm sure it is,' Trina said.

One of the reasons Trina married Graham was for his logical, practical way of seeing the world. She first met him on a weekend away with her university friends. They had taken a site on the top of a cliff overlooking Bass Strait. The wind was howling when they arrived and heavy raindrops pelted their faces as they began erecting the tent. Putting it up seemed impossible as she and her friend, Tamra, fought to keep the fly from blowing off the cliff. Finally they managed to strap it down, but the flimsy poles buckled against the force of the wind.

Graham and his mates were at the adjoining campsite. They sat under a tarpaulin they'd strung up between two trees, drinking beer and watching with amusement as the two girls struggled against nature. Graham finally went over to help.

'You know what you've done wrong?' he said, holding his stubbie in one hand and a joint in the other. His brow wrinkled in seriousness, though his eyes were laughing.

Full of independence and ideals of feminism, the girls assured him they knew exactly what they were doing and were managing quite well on their own.

'Here, hold this,' he said to Tamra, passing her his lukewarm beer.

Graham worked on the tent as though it were a sculpture he was carefully moulding. He turned the tent around forty five degrees and told Trina to pass him the pegs.

'But we want to be facing the ocean,' Trina insisted as Graham hammered in a peg.

'You'll be getting a real close, open air view of it if you run it that way. You want to keep dry, don't you?' he said, continuing his handiwork.

Trina glanced over at her friend, who merely shrugged and took a sip of Graham's beer.

The next day Graham and Trina walked along the cliff, looking out at the ocean. Trina marvelled at the strength and size of the waves as Graham showed her where the rips were. Trina thought it odd that he tell her this in the middle of winter, when she had no intention of even paddling her feet in the water. It was as though he wanted to explain everything to her so she didn't get hurt. Though in later years Trina fought with Graham over the way he always had to explain things, as though she was incapable of looking after herself, it was one of the things she loved about him. He protected her from becoming idealistic, and Trina was glad for this. It kept her from expecting too much.

'Which way?' Graham asked.

Trina was pulled back into the moment as they arrived on the outskirts of Loch Sport. The small wooden sign welcoming them to the township was slanted on one side so that the arrows pointing the way to the town's attractions directed you into the wetlands.

'Either way,' Trina said.

Graham frowned but turned left. He couldn't understand that whether you turned left or right, you were still going to wind up in the same place. But that's what amused Trina the most about Loch Sport. Either way you were right. Either way you ended up at the bakery, the motel or the beach. Even though the arrows pointed to specific features of the town, it didn't really matter whether you followed them or not. You still got to them, eventually.

Trina was glad Graham turned left. It took them along the residential part of the sparse township. The small, unfenced fibro and weatherboard holiday houses looked the same as Trina remembered. Box-shaped abodes, with slanted roofs and front decks. They were painted in beiges, greens and pale blues; tourists' attempts at blending their houses in with the scenery. Trees, dirt and water. Too much water for such a small place. Maybe that was why Trina hated it so much. It was enclosed by water—the still, murky water of the lake; the wild, frothing, blue-green water of the ocean; the stagnant, shallow water of the wetlands and the pools of water congealing in the front yards of the low blocks of land and infrequently visited homes. The road became smooth as Graham drove along the lake's edge, where most of the permanent residents lived. The only way to tell these apart was from the lawns and plants that were in place of the sand and yellow, red and purple wildflowers that adorned the front yards of holiday houses. They passed the pub, which had been repainted in popular beach colours. Trina felt a sudden urge to tell Graham to keep going, straight past the lake and back out of Loch Sport, but she remained silent.

After passing the houses that dotted the landscape they turned in at the boat launch, stopping just short of the ramp.

'This it?' Graham asked, sounding pleased at himself for following the appropriate signs successfully, without any guidance from Trina.

Trina wiped the condensation away from the window and stared out.

'That's odd,' she said.

'What?'

'It looks like a light's on.'

'You want me to go ahead and check it out?'

'No, we'll both go. I'm sure it's nothing.'

'Probably just kids. Still, I think I should go have a look first.'

'No!'

Trina felt a strange sense of ownership of the houseboat. Though it was her mother's and she'd vowed years ago that she would never step foot on it again, she now wanted to be the first to touch the wooden decking. She wrenched open the car door and raced along the foreshore of the lake to the houseboat. The familiar smell of algae and rotted fish filled her nostrils. The feel of rough sand and tiny pebbles that found their way into her runners was all too familiar.

She didn't give herself time to notice the deterioration of the houseboat's exterior. Instead she swung open the screen door, its rusted hinges creaking. Standing before her was Lauren, folding a sheet across her torso, ghost-like. Her blonde bob moved up and down as she worked. The silence that filled the musty air was soon shattered as Lauren turned, sensing another presence in the small space. The air became heavy and bustling with noise. Unspoken words shot from the walls, the bed, the table. The cook top burst into angry flame. Dust motes floated up, down, back and forward, trying to dodge the arrows shooting through their air. The gentle lapping of the waves was drowned out as the sisters' exchange took place. Neither spoke. It was Graham who interrupted the battle.

'I'll just put these down here for now,' he said, having arrived closely behind his wife.

Trina remained still, standing opposite Lauren. Graham dropped the bags heavily to the floor and held out his hand to Lauren, but she didn't allow her concentration to be broken. Graham glanced at Trina but she didn't notice him. Her eyes were still locked on Lauren's.

'I'll go get the rest of our things. Back in a minute,' Graham said.

Trina began shifting from foot to foot, uncertain, as Lauren had already marked her territory, her scent strong in the air.

'What are you doing here?' Trina demanded, trying to get an even standing.

'What do *you* think I'm doing here?'

The question was rhetorical but Trina answered anyway, mainly because she didn't know what else to say.

'She asked you to clean the place up. Make it nice. So you'd want to buy it yourself. You'll need a mop, a broom, a few planks of wood and nails for the decking. Oh, and don't forget to take some detergent. The linen will need washing…'

Lauren took over. 'You'll need some bleach for the sheets.' She tossed the sheet she had removed from the bunk onto the floor.

'This was deliberate. She set us up,' Trina said, as though Lauren were somehow responsible.

'She's ill. Doped up on drugs 24/7. She forgets her own name half the time.'

'No, she doesn't forget her name. She doesn't forget anything,' Trina said.

'I didn't come here to argue with you.'

'I didn't come here to *see* you.'

Trina knew her words, her tone of voice were childish. Irrational. She was surprised at how seeing Lauren made her feel twelve years old again and she hated her all the more for it. Trina tried to avoid her sister's gaze, but she had never been able to ignore her presence. She wore that same expression Trina remembered. The one that told her she was guilty. That it was all her fault. The one that said, *how could you do this to me?*

9

Trina remembered the first time she'd seen that look. She was only five years old. The sisters were almost identical at that age, but it wasn't so much their physical features that made people unsure of who was who. It was the way they held their heads on the same angle when they listened to their mother talk. It was the way they spread their arms wide when their daddy came home from work, waiting for him to pick them up, one in each arm, and spin them around. It was the way they moved their tongues from side to side along their red lips when they were colouring in or trying to work out a jigsaw puzzle. For a small part of their lives they each saw themselves as one half of a whole. 'There's no Punch without Judy,' their daddy would always say. Although neither of them knew who Punch and Judy were, they knew what he meant, and whenever he said it they would press their foreheads together, giggling into each other's faces.

Once they started school, Trina felt something shift. Suddenly it wasn't Trina-and-Lauren anymore, all melded into one. It was now Trina *and* Lauren. Suddenly red and yellow no longer made orange because the colours wouldn't blend. And so their paintings didn't have the rich texture and brightness about them anymore.

Sweat and tears rolled down their mother's face as she waved them goodbye on their first day at school. Trina and Lauren held slippery hands and watched their mother fade into the distance. The hot asphalt bore through the soles of Trina's tan lace ups. She dragged Lauren by the hand, away from their mother, as much in eagerness to escape the heat burning her scalp as in excitement about what she was about to discover at the top of that concrete stairway. Trina could feel the resistance from her sister.

She leant towards her and whispered, 'Guess what?'

'What?'

'I saw Mum put donuts in our lunchboxes. And, they've got sprinkles on them.'

'What colour?'

'Pink.'

Trina found herself at the top of the stairs, still holding Lauren's drier hand, and she knew it was hers that was wet now. The corridor was long and she'd never seen so many doors. And they were all the same; dark green with a small window too high up for her to peek through. Lauren looked relaxed, assured by her sister's confidence. Trina knew Lauren was waiting for her to show her the next step, but she didn't know what it was. She thought once she reached the top of the stairs she had made it. She was there. But now there were all these doors and she didn't know which one was theirs to go through.

'Trina and Lauren Moore?'

'Yes!' Trina said.

'I'll take you to your classrooms.'

Trina and Lauren followed the smiley woman who had called them by name down the corridor, still clutching each other's hands. The smiley woman stopped and the girls stopped behind her. She pointed to one of the green doors. It had a big number four on it.

'Now, which one of you is Lauren?'

'Me,' Lauren said, almost whispering.

'Well, Lauren,' the smiley woman said, crouching down to her level, 'this is your classroom. Your teacher's name is Miss Crow.'

She reached out to take her hand and Trina felt the grip on her own hand tighten.

'Come on, dear. You'll see your sister at playtime.'

Trina was the one who finally pulled her slippery hand out of Lauren's and the smiley woman's cold hand quickly replaced it. Trina stood in the corridor as Lauren was led into the classroom. She watched her sister's ponytail swishing from side to side with each step, until finally it disappeared behind the green door, and she wished she hadn't been the first to let go. She could never retrieve the moment she separated herself from Lauren. Once she had broken that bond it could never be repaired and it was Trina who suffered the loss the most, or at least that was how it seemed to her. What she didn't see was Lauren searching for Trina in the school grounds, and being unable to concentrate in class because she was afraid of being alone. What Trina *did* see was Lauren adjusting well to school life and leaving her behind. She saw her laugh with friends, play in the schoolyard, and ignore her.

The moment the bell rang for play lunch on that first day,

Trina was out of the classroom and waiting at the bottom of the stairs for Lauren. She scanned blue and white checked uniforms. She saw pale legs, suntanned legs, freckled legs. She compared pulled up socks, short socks, scrunched socks, but she couldn't pick Lauren out of the blur of uniformity. Trina sat alone on the bench beside the stairway and chewed on her pink donut. The treat she had been so looking forward to sat in the pit of her stomach and when the bell rang for the second time she reluctantly made her way back to class, hoping to catch a glimpse of Lauren racing to catch up with her. But Lauren was nowhere to be seen.

When the girls were picked up from school, Trina sat quietly, a painting on her lap, while Lauren told her mother all about the friends she had made.

'And you should see Rachel's hair, Mum. It's cut real short and kind of sits under. She calls it a bob. Can I have my hair cut like that Mum?' Lauren said.

'What about you, Trina? How was your day?' her mother asked.

'It was all right.'

'What did you do?'

'Not much.'

'Well, you must have done something.'

'At lunchtime I played hopscotch with Emma and Rachel,' Lauren interrupted. 'Rachel's really good at it too.'

'You were s'posed to meet me at the bottom of the stairs,' Trina said quietly.

'I forgot.'

But Trina knew Lauren hadn't forgotten, and so did their mother. And they both noticed the shift. Trina began to spend more and more time in her bedroom, sitting on her bed and staring at her wizard picture, wishing he could cast a magic spell and change things back to the way they used to be, before there was any such thing as school. Lauren's conversation about friends and games and lunchtimes made Trina's silence easy. Trina watched Lauren envelop the change and move along with it. She wanted a sparkly pencil-case like Emma and coloured contact on her books like Suzie. But most of all she wanted to have her hair cut into a bob, like her new best friend Rachel. She no longer wanted to look like Trina. She didn't want to wear the same clothes or have the same hairstyle. Trina had felt Lauren's hand slip out of hers and she wished again that she hadn't been the first to let go. Perhaps then she wouldn't have become the one who felt responsible for them both.

It wasn't until several weeks later that Trina first saw Lauren's *how could you do this to me?* look. It was a day when Trina saw her mother talking to Miss Crow that their hands were truly pried apart. Trina couldn't hear what was being said, but she could see her mother's eyes go dark and she could see her mother's muscles contracting and she suddenly seemed much smaller than Miss Crow.

'Get in the car,' was all her mother said when she'd finished being shrunk by Miss Crow.

Trina looked at Lauren for answers, but Lauren wouldn't look back at her, and without seeing her eyes Trina had no way of knowing what the meeting with Miss Crow was about. It wasn't until after the long journey home that Trina found out the reason her mother had shrunk.

When they got home Lauren and Trina placed themselves

in front of the television. They knew to avoid their mother by being silent, and keeping occupied, when she was in one of 'those moods'. Above the sound of the wildlife show, with its commentary about mutton-bird migratory patterns, Trina could hear her mother in the kitchen. A plate banged against the bench. Two pots crashed together. The fridge door opened and shut. Opened and shut. A cup smashed to the ground. Footsteps grew louder. Their mother appeared in the doorway, a piece of china in her hand. Trina noticed she had grown back to her full size while she was in the kitchen.

'Who put this cup away?'

Trina and Lauren continued to stare at the television screen.

'Who was it?'

Still, neither answered.

'For the last time, who put this cup away?'

Silence.

'Get to your rooms. Both of you!' she screamed.

Trina got up and ran to her room, shutting the door behind her. She heard Lauren's door close after hers.

Trina stared fixedly at her wizard as though he could magically whisk her away, but eventually she heard her door open.

'Come with me.'

Trina followed her mother into the bathroom. Slamming the lid of the toilet seat, she said, 'Sit down.'

Trina obediently sat. She heard her mother open the bathroom cabinet, rustle around, and close it again. A pair of hairdressing scissors appeared, clutched tightly in her mother's hand. Trina frowned, wondering why she would choose now to trim her hair. She said nothing, knowing better than to argue when her mother was angry.

But when Trina felt the first chop and looked down, she saw long, dark blonde hair covering the tiles. She felt her hair, felt its missing-ness, and burst into tears. She screamed at her mother to stop, as though she could somehow reverse what was done.

'Sit still or you'll end up with none,' her mother said. 'And don't cry about it. If you two hadn't played your little twin games in the playground I wouldn't need to do this, would I?'

'I don't know about any twin games,' Trina whispered.

'Miss Crow told me all about you two, trying to trick the teachers on yard duty.'

'But I didn't…'

Trina felt the side of the blade against the nape of her neck and knew arguing would only make things worse, so she sat still while her mother cut her hair into a neat bob.

10

Lauren lay on the small bunk, unable to sleep even though she was exhausted from the turmoil of her return to Loch Sport. She remembered that the bunk had felt too small for her in her teenage years. Where as a child the narrow mattress and short length had been comforting in comparison to her larger bed at home, as she grew older she began to outgrow it. She remembered how cramped it was, as she could no longer toss and turn freely. She'd imagined it was similar to how a lanky school mate might feel, trying to fit long legs under a short and narrow desk.

Lying in the bed now felt the same, only it was intensified by the fact that she'd gained weight since her teenage years and the mattress was now sinking in the centre. Lauren pushed a lumpy pillow with the palm of her hand as though she could knead it into a comfortable shape. Frustrated, she sat up to adjust it, hitting her head on the metal springs from the top bunk. She leant forward only to be pulled back again. Her hair was caught in the metal prongs, holding her in a semi-seated position. Lauren tugged roughly at her hair, not realising how many strands the springs had captured and now pulled at her scalp. If she'd had the patience and wasn't already angry she would have taken the time to unravel her hair, but she continued to wrench her head forward until she was free, minus a chunk of hair that remained twisted among the coils.

Lauren lay back down on the sinking mattress and stared at the hair held in the spring's vice-like grip. Tears began to fill her eyes, and she let the throbbing in the back of her head take the blame. It was good to have an excuse to let some of the tension out, though she did it silently, not wanting Trina to hear her. As she lay there in the darkness, listening to the lap of water against the side of the boat and the quiet echo of Trina and Graham whispering to each other from the opposite end of the boat, she wondered why she had agreed to stay. She told herself she should have grabbed her belongings and driven back to her unit the moment she saw Trina. But when Trina began arguing she found herself fighting back.

'There's no need for you to be here,' Lauren had said, trying to sound accommodating in her urge to get her sister to leave.

'I'm bloody well not going home now, am I?'

'You'd be home by dinnertime.'

'My arse is numb. I feel like shit.'

'She threw up on the way here,' Graham said by way of explanation. Trina glared at him. She had never liked weakness, least of all in herself.

'And anyway, Graham and I could knock it over much quicker with the two of us.'

'I've brought a heap of tools along,' Graham said by way of agreement, and Lauren realised it was two against one.

'I promised her,' Lauren said quietly. 'I'm not going.'

'Neither am I.'

'Right, it's settled then. It's ridiculous for anyone to leave. Tonight at least. Trina and I can take the double and you can take the bunks. If you're happy with that of course, Lauren?'

'I guess,' Lauren had found herself saying.

'I'll get the gear out for a barbie. I'm starving.'

Somehow Graham's logical reasoning had won, yet it didn't seem so logical to her. Still, she was unable to come up with another solution. She liked to think she and Trina were opposites in every way. But if there was one similarity between them, she had to admit they could be as stubborn as one another and when they locked horns neither was able to back away. She had decided to keep conversation polite and neutral, get to work, and get out of there as soon as the houseboat was ready. But the strain of avoiding each other's strong presence was already getting to her. Her toes caressed the cold metal bed frame at the base of the bunk. She knew she was not going to sleep. Thoughts whirled in her head and she saw spirals of colour when she closed her eyes. The sound of Trina and Graham whispering seemed to grow louder and deeper and the constant lapping of water no longer had the same calming effect as it had when she was a child.

11

All Gisella had now were her memories. They came in a symphony, as though each memory was a separate instrument and together they made an orchestra. High notes and low notes, forte and piano, sharps and flats, high pitch and low pitch, fast and slow, heavy and light. She could control the sounds by will, but which instruments played and which remained silent, or in the background, she could not. If she could choose she'd select the harp in the early evening when her meal had been half eaten and the sun shone yellow through her small window. She'd pick the drums when the nurses rolled by her half open doorway delivering meals, pills and injections. She'd favour the flute when her daughter Lauren entered the room, her arms carrying fresh clean clothes and a fast food box filled with soggy chips and a lukewarm chicken drumstick.

But she could not choose and the memories were not nearly so kind to her. They came to torment her, to torture her already bedraggled body. They picked their moments to come tearing into her heart, her mind, and all she could do was try to control the tone of them. Even this was difficult. So she tried to push them back by filling her mind with the present, always the present, never the past. She spoke of television and trashy magazines and the man in the room next to hers, who coughed in his sleep. She drowned the orchestra out with how cold it was during the night and how uncomfortable the pillows were and how slow the nurses were to respond to her calls. What if something should happen to her? She'd be dead by the time they got to her. She may as well be living back at home. At least she could do as she pleased there. At least she didn't have to listen to the coughing man's grandchildren screeching through the wall when she was trying to take a nap. She didn't want to complain. Really she didn't. But she had to do something to drown out the noise. And what else was there to talk about? Not much happened in her present. There wasn't any future. So what else was there?

It had been three months and twenty-one days since she'd been carted into this place. *Hell before salvation.* The nurses found her definitions of the palliative care unit highly amusing, but Gisella didn't. She didn't know she'd be waiting so long, alone with her memories. Alone to mull over every single event of her life.

Gisella reached over to her side table, opened the drawer and removed an envelope from beneath her folded nightgowns. She held it against her chest until she fell asleep. Days, weeks, months had passed her by and still her heart beat strongly against the envelope. It was not long before her snores filled the empty room, the letter settling beside her as her fingers relaxed.

12

Lauren stood on the deck, watching long shadowy fingers stretch out and retract as the boat gently lifted and sank. She held the flaky railing tightly in both hands, lack of sleep making her feel detached from her reality.

'Looks like it's going to be another hot one.' Graham stepped up to the railing beside Lauren, two thick shadows now darkening the water.

She continued to stare out as the clouds shifted across the sky, uncovering the sun, and her eyes narrowed against the glare. The sun's rays reflected off the lake in shards that somehow seemed to penetrate her eyes but not Graham's, filling her head with heat and light.

'Might have to make an early start on fixing the boat up, before it gets too hot,' Graham said. 'We should be able to knock it over by Tuesday.'

'Tuesday?'

'Yeah. I mean it's stupid for anyone to go home now. Now we're all here.'

'Less stupid than Trina and I working on this thing together?'

'And me. This boat's a mess.'

'No, no it's not. It just needs a patch up. I can do this on my own you know? That's what I thought I was doing anyway.'

'Look, I'm no tradie. I'll be the first to admit that. But I've got the basic skills. This boat needs a complete overhaul. You need me. You need us.'

Lauren looked down at the rotting timber. She couldn't pretend she hadn't noticed the orange stains of rust, the warped linoleum, the broken screens. She doubted she could even get the thing started in this state. She realised she was quickly running out of excuses. Maybe he was right. She did need the help. Maybe it was time to take some—her sister owed her that much at least.

'You need a man's strength,' Graham persisted. 'How are you going to get those planks up by yourself for one?'

'Okay, okay. I know. You're right.'

'We'd better get started then.'

'Yeah, I guess,' Lauren sighed. 'I just don't know how we're going to stay on this boat together for three days without killing each other first.'

She waited for Graham to leave, but he just stood there looking at her. Contemplating her. She had meant that as an afterthought. She knew that's where it should have remained, as a thought.

'It's a shame you guys don't get along. I couldn't imagine life without Rob. He's my half-brother. We hang out together all the time. You know, a few beers at the local. Fishing in summer. That kind of stuff.'

Shit, he wanted a D and M now?

'Good for you.'

'I mean if anything happened to one of us, God forbid, I

know he'd look after things, you know?'

'I'm sure I don't.' She realised it was up to her to do the leaving. 'I'd better get a start on the inside. The walls will need a good scrub before we can even think about painting.'

Graham's pestering was starting to make her headache worse. She wondered if he spoke like this to Trina. She guessed not. Perhaps he saw her as a way to mend the family. He obviously didn't know much about their history or he wouldn't even be trying.

As she turned to leave she felt pinpricks of pain hitting the inside of her temples and she squinted her eyes, pressing her hand against her forehead. When she opened her eyes again, bright silver flecks danced across the lake, floating over the shadows that had elongated, reaching to the centre of the lake. She longed to dunk her head beneath the surface of the water, the place she often went to when she was younger, where there was no heat and no sound.

'Are you all right?' Graham asked.

'Yes, just a bit of a headache, that's all.'

'I'm going to get some timber and nails from Sale. Can I get you anything?'

'No, I'm fine. Nothing a couple of Panadol won't fix.'

'Right. I'll be off then.'

Lauren nodded, then waited until Graham's footsteps stopped echoing in her brain. When the air was still again, she stepped down onto the pontoon, the water tickling its edges. She lay down on her stomach and hung her arms over the edge, dangling them in the water. Wriggling further forward, she let her head fall forward until it too was immersed in the cool water. She held her breath until her senses were numb, except for the salty taste of the water. But despite her attempts she could not block out her past any longer. Loch Sport had reached out its shadow arms and enveloped her, consuming her in its dark clutches.

She was taken back to the day she first met Hal. She could still see the glint of his eye that had made her smile, but strangely also made her wary. It was one of mischievousness and it mirrored a side of herself she had always wanted to express but was unable to. Fear prevented her from taking a risk and Hal's inherent desire to do so allowed them to quickly become friends. Their friendship had many of the expected elements; fun, laughter, an understanding and sharing of aspects of their lives others couldn't comprehend. But in other ways it wasn't like most friendships Lauren had known. She'd not had many to draw comparisons with, but she knew there was something different about theirs and it often made her step back when she feared she'd revealed too much. She could see Hal become annoyed, frustrated when she changed her mind midway through a thought she'd begun to express. Perhaps that was why Trina became Hal's girlfriend and not her. Not that she ever saw him in that way. Something she didn't understand in herself prevented her from trusting herself to him.

Hal and Lauren had first met at the Loch Sport General Store. Hal had just begun working weekends behind the register. His dad owned the mini-mart in the centre of the small town. The small brick building lay exactly midway across the rows of houses and vacant blocks that edged the lake. It was also the same distance away from each of the two boat launches. As the only place to buy groceries, milk, bread and margarine would cost twice what you would pay in the next closest town of Sale. Theoretically, the locals would avoid paying such ridiculous prices and stock up on everything they needed on their monthly visits to Sale, leaving the tourists to be ripped off on their weekend visits in the summer months. In reality, the locals frequented the store, under the pretence of forgetting some essential item for their refrigerator, when they actually came to catch up on the local gossip.

Of course, Lauren's mother was far too sensible for such nonsense, and more pertinently only came for the summer and was therefore not considered a local and not considered worthy of hearing about the time Mrs Franklin caught Mr Franklin having it off with one of their staff members on the front counter of their coffee lounge. However, on this occasion Lauren's mother had forgotten to buy margarine in Sale and sent Lauren to get it.

The moment she entered the store she noticed eyes following her. She self-consciously walked through the narrow aisles, searching for the cold section. She'd unknowingly wandered past it twice before she found herself looking in his direction.

'What you after?'

'Marg.'

'Right behind you.'

'Oh yeah, thanks.'

Lauren placed the small tub on the counter, trying to ignore the smirk, the look that told her she was just a silly tourist. What would she know? Hal put the container in a plastic bag. Lauren handed him a crisp note. He took it between his thick fingers and placed it in the till, before handing her a handful of coins in return. He'd short-changed her. She could tell it was deliberate. That gleam in his eye revealed all. Though she wanted to mouth a protest she found herself unable to. She accepted the change.

Back then Lauren had confided in Trina about all her inhibitions. Her fears of the world. Of people. Of asserting herself. She had no need to keep a teenager's diary. All her secrets lay hidden inside Trina. She knew Trina didn't do the same in return. In fact, Lauren doubted she knew very much at all about how Trina felt about anything. At the same time, she knew she could trust Trina completely. And that had been enough for her.

'He did what?' Trina said, incredulous.

'It wasn't much,' Lauren protested.

'That's not the point. You sure you didn't work out the maths wrong? You're not very good at maths, you know?'

'I'm sure.'

'You shouldn't let people tramp all over you. You have to be more assertive.'

Lauren's eyes begin to well. She wished she were as strong as Trina.

'Don't worry. I've got an idea,' Trina said, grinning wildly.

The following day, at Trina's insistence, they dressed identically in matching jeans and white t-shirts. They even tied their hair back in the same ponytail. Trina sent Lauren into the general store first.

'Hi,' she said timidly.

'You again,' Hal said, his eyes dancing with amusement.

Lauren felt her face redden. Trina had told her a few things she could say to get them talking. 'Many up here these holidays?'

'Many like you, you mean?' he said.

'Yeah, I guess,' Lauren found herself laughing softly.

'Too many,' he said.

'Must bring in a few bucks for you guys though,' Lauren said, feeling her confidence grow and expand.

'Few more hours I have to spend stuck in here instead of out on the water.'

From the corner of her eye, Lauren saw Trina sneak in and hide behind a shelf filled with canned goods that sat growing dust.

Lauren shrugged. 'Bread?'

Hal pointed to the back corner. Lauren casually picked a loaf of fresh white bread, delivered from the bakery up the road. It was still warm in her hands. Hal placed it in a bag and handed it back to her, the loaf already sweating inside its plastic encasement. Lauren smiled as she paid and then left the store. She peered in the front window; Hal's back was turned to her, and she watched as Trina appeared from inside the store holding a carton of milk. Hal's eyes widened. He turned his head to look out the front door as if to find her. But he acted calmly as he placed the milk in another plastic bag, took Trina's money and incredulously watched her leave.

Trina tapped Lauren and they ran off, laughing as they had frequently done when they were children at the shared joke.

'Sucked in,' Trina said.

'Sucked in,' Lauren repeated.

Over several weekends, Lauren and Trina repeated their trick. Hal became so confused they began to feel sorry for him. His brow furrowed deeper and his skin paled as he mulled over the most likely scenario: was he going crazy or was he being visited by a ghost? But Hal proved smarter than to believe in ghosts or his own insanity, and after deciding at some point that neither situation was reasonable he got a friend to take over his position behind the counter while he strode up the hill in search of his answer. And he got it. Not one but two Laurens sat by the side of the road, their arms wrapped around each other as tears of laughter streamed down their faces.

Lauren was the first to notice him. His hands, balled up into hard fists, were held firmly on his hips. His legs were spread out wide and appeared cemented to the ground. It was as if he was trying to become larger than Lauren and Trina put together as he waited to gain their attention. He stood staring, his eyes ablaze. For a brief moment, Lauren felt a sickness in her stomach and wanted to crawl into the tea-tree, away from the confrontation. Instead she turned her eyes away, secure in the presence of her sister. She continued to laugh, tapping her sister's arm to alert her to Hal. Trina looked over, but by this time Hal's body had softened and though he had at first been angry, she was pleased that he was quickly caught up in their laughter by the side of the road. Still, something about his initial reaction made her wary, and excited, like a child handed a new puppy.

13

Trina felt the weight of their bodies pushing against the lightness of the houseboat as it gently lifted and sank on the water. She put together a light breakfast of toast and locally preserved jams. Coffee brewed on the small stove. Bread toasted under the grill. She enjoyed cooking simply. She automatically made coffee for Lauren the same way as she made it for herself.

'Thank you,' Lauren said with polite tension.

Graham lathered jam over his toast. 'So what's the plan?'

'I can take the linen down to the laundromat this morning,' Trina said.

'No, I'll take it. I bundled it all up last night,' Lauren protested.

'Fine, you take it. I don't care,' Trina said, unable to prevent herself from sounding childish.

'Do you want to do the sanding?' Graham asked.

'I hate sanding,' Trina said.

'I'll sand,' Lauren said.

'You already insisted on going to the laundromat,' Trina argued.

'I can do both.'

'You're making me sound like I'm not doing anything,' Trina protested.

'You're not.'

'Excuse me...'

'I mean, you're not *yet*. God knows, there's plenty to do.'

'Why don't you pull the fly screens off? Some are okay. The ripped ones I can replace,' Graham interjected.

'I'm not your bloody lackey,' Trina said, turning her anger to Graham.

'Fine, do what you like. I was just trying to be helpful.'

Trina wondered how their plan for fixing up the houseboat had quickly become so impossible. It should have been simple and straightforward. Despite her conscious desire to be reasonable and mature, she found herself becoming heated over the small things. Finally, as always, Graham had come to her rescue and made the decisions for them.

'Okay, let's just do this the logical way. I need to take the bilge pump in later to be replaced. I'll pull it out while you girls nut out between you what you want done with the place. I guess we'll have to wash the walls down before they can be painted. I don't think there's much point trying to clean that old lino. Might as well pull it all up and then think about colours.' He turned to Lauren. 'I'm useless at colour coordination. Just ask Trina. That's definitely women's business.'

Trina found her sister nodding agreement in the same way she did, as though they were connected to a wire. At first she thought it was a sign they were the same after all, but she soon realised it was just because her sister was equally as determined as her not to launch an assault on the other. Lauren knew as well as she that their fighting energy had been sapped from them years ago.

After having their day pre-organised by Graham, the rest of the morning had seemed simple as Trina busied herself getting ready. Showering, dressing and cleaning her teeth took longer than usual though, as she tried to avoid closeness with Lauren in the small space. But she knew she had to face her sister eventually.

She peered through the flimsy curtains at her sister submerging her head in the water. The pounding in her head had disappeared to a dull ache since taking the pain relievers Graham dependably left her. She watched thick droplets of water etch the decking as Lauren bent her neck back. It surprised her how her sister's movements replicated those she had made as a teenager so exactly. Although her hair had been much longer then, Lauren still leaned back at the same angle, with her elbows slightly bent and her wrists flexed back, so her tiny blue veins were exposed. But despite the physical similarities, Trina's feelings had changed. Where once she had enjoyed waking to this image of Lauren, it now filled her heart with a burning, a longing for something lost that could not be retrieved. Why their mother had decided to place them together in the same setting that had driven them apart was beyond her comprehension. She should know they could never work things out. Not after what had happened. She watched Lauren stare out at the lake, oblivious to the drops of water that fell from her wet hair, soaking the back of her shirt. She wondered what Lauren was thinking, what made her get that faraway look like she was trying to distance herself from the place she stood in. That look frustrated Trina and angered her because it was so impenetrable.

'Lauren!'

Trina watched as her sister's back muscles tightened beneath her shirt with fright.

'Where'd Graham get to?'

Lauren's neck elongated and her eyes narrowed as she saw her try to make out the words. Trina flung open the side door and stepped onto the drops of water that had settled on the decking, leaving behind the wavy imprint of her sandal.

'I said, where's Graham?'

'Oh, he's gone to get the new bilge pump. For the bow or something.'

'Already?'

She knew Graham's decision to get the pump had little to do with his interest in fixing up the boat and more to do with his warped idea that she just needed some time alone with her sister.

'I guess we'd better get started on this place then,' Trina said.

'Yeah, we'll both want to get out of here ASAP.'

Trina didn't offer any argument, knowing the statement was unnecessary—they knew as well as each other they were eager to leave Loch Sport, and one another, as soon as they could.

Trina went back inside and tried to quickly find tasks that needed her urgent attention. She had her head stuck inside the kitchenette cupboards by the time Lauren had dried off and entered the cabin. Her sister was doing the same, trying to find a task that would avoid contact with her. She concentrated vehemently on scrubbing the cupboard doors. Lauren displayed equal fervour in washing down the windows. The silence of the unspoken was almost unbearable.

Trina scrubbed harder and faster in an attempt to increase the noise level inside the houseboat. But even that didn't seem enough. She plugged in the portable CD player she had brought along and switched it on, turning the volume up loud so to disturb the silence.

For some reason she couldn't comprehend, the music seemed to dislodge the fragments of conversation hanging loosely from her vocal chords. And despite her willingness not to, she found herself speaking. Not in silent thoughts, but aloud.

'These cupboard liners are a prick to get off,' she said, peeling off a thick piece of bright green contact.

'No wonder. They've been there forever,' Lauren responded.

'The seventies were so ugly.'

'Ugly. Not as ugly as the eighties though.'

'Do you remember that horrid hairstyle Mum used to have?'

'Not the bat wings?'

'Yeah, the bat wings. Hideous,' Trina agreed.

'Not as bad as the spike.'

'Or the perm.'

'I noticed you grew your hair,' Lauren said.

'Soon as I left home,' Trina said.

'I thought the bob suited you.'

'I never wanted a bob.'

'Oh?'

Trina didn't want to delve into explanations about the past.

'Have you got a scraper? It's ruining my fingernails pulling this off by hand,' Trina said.

'In the boot.' Lauren tossed her the car keys.

Trina went outside, breathed in the salt air. She hated the smell of the place. Stagnant. She unlocked the boot to Lauren's car. At least there was conversation at last. She hated silences. She always tried to fill them. Lauren was always the quiet one; while she often seemed content to sit and ponder, even in the company of others, Trina believed any words were better than none. Working in PR was her perfect world. Non-stop gabbing was essential, and essential to her. She waltzed back inside.

'You've still got that old bomb? God, wasn't that your first car? I can't believe it's still running.'

'Yeah, I guess it has been that long. I've never really thought about it.'

'You should get yourself a new car. It's better to have something reliable.'

'It's never broken down on me.'

Trina started scraping, scarcely noticing the mood was shifting as the shadows lengthened across the houseboat.

'Don't you worry that it will though?'

'Well, in case you hadn't noticed, I don't have piles of money.'

'I couldn't go without my lifestyle. I never understood why you chose this life for yourself.'

'What, of poverty?' Lauren said sarcastically.

'You know what I mean. Giving up everything for a woman who tortured you all your life.'

Lauren threw her squeegee to the ground and spun around.

'I don't see things the same way as you do, Trina. It may seem to you I've sacrificed, but really I just decided to give instead of take.'

'Well, I decided to live. Not to escape from the world by becoming a martyr.'

'Then why did you come here?'

'You wouldn't understand.'

'Actually I do. I still know you better than you think. You thought if you did something for Mum it would make up for all the years you weren't there for her. You think by coming here you don't have to feel guilty that you left me to look after her. You think I like cleaning up after her? You think I like watching her slowly die in front of me? You really believe I chose this life for myself? No, you've decided to see it that way because it's easier.'

Trina felt her anger rise quickly. She told herself she was furious for being accused of such lies. She had only been to visit last week.

'No, it was your choice to allow her the satisfaction of dying in front of you. She's ill because she chose to be. She's ill because she's enjoying seeing you suffer. If anyone's failing to care for her it's you. Without you she wouldn't be dying. There'd be no point.'

Trina watched as Lauren melted before her eyes. She listened to Lauren's voice echo and disappear and re-emerge again but she didn't hear what she was saying. She could only hear fragments, reaching out and sliding away again. Then Lauren faded into shadow as she walked away from her. Trina stared at the long shadow of her sister, stretching along the side wall of the houseboat as she made her way to the pontoon. Lauren's shadow body elongated and retracted with the rise and fall of the boat. Her narrow shadow arms and even narrower shadow fingers stretched out in long tendrils against the cream facade. Her fingers bent and twisted out of shape as the shadow hit the windowsills. Trina wanted to grab those fingers and pull them back into shape. She wanted to give them strength and solidity but she could not grab on for they were only an illusion. Instead, Lauren dived into the lake, confirming the friendship they'd held as children had long gone.

Lauren's head disappeared beneath the water, followed by her torso, her arms, her feet as she entered the cool depths of the lake. Trina called out, but her sister was already too far away to hear. The even movements of left arm and right arm penetrated the surface before disappearing again beneath the water. She stared as her sister swam across the lake into the darker, murkier, wavier waters and began to regret she'd begun the conversation.

Trina felt a tap on her shoulder. Ridiculously, she first thought it was Lauren, until she turned to find her husband with one arm loaded up. She didn't know whether to laugh or cry at him, miniaturised by timber and paint.

'Got a few extra things on the way back,' he said by way of explanation.

'Fuck!'

Graham answered her call, dropped the timber, and without explanation wrapped her in his comforting arms.

14

Gisella hated the nights the most. It was too loud and she was left alone with no one to distract her. Little distraction meant the orchestra began to play louder and louder until she could no longer block the sound out with the television or complaints to the nurses about the food. Alone, one night, Gisella reached over to the bedside table, pulled open the top drawer with the small strength she still had in her weak arm, and took out the yellowed and crinkled envelope. As she turned the envelope over and over in her hands, like she had more times than she knew, she found herself replaying in her mind the day Christian left.

She could still see that day as clearly as she did the thin scar across his forehead. In the early days, after they made love, she would rest her head on her elbow and, with her free hand, run her finger along the marred skin. She used to tell him it gave him an extra wrinkle—an extra year of worry. She would ask him to explain again how he got the scar; from running smack bang into the corrugated iron roofing that hung precariously over his father's homemade shed. 'But I were jus' a little tacker then. An' I were ever so careful after that.' Gisella always laughed when he told the scar story; no one could be more uncoordinated than him if they tried.

That had been in the early days. Gisella liked the expression, 'early days'. It reminded her of an Easter chick. Newly hatched, with fresh eyes on the world and a keenness for the discoveries that awaited. Like wakening early. Gisella always woke early, when the sky was the deepest of blues, so you can barely tell it isn't dark. She always awoke with the freshness of a newborn chick. A cherished feeling, when she was still groggy from sleep but hadn't yet realised where she was in the world. There is no past, or future, only today. But as the fogginess of sleep lifted, Gisella would become aware that the present can't exist without memory of the past and premonition for the future. And so she remembered that day, seeing the glaringly white envelope lying flat against the deep brown stain of the tabletop. She had read her name, scrawled hastily with a blue ballpoint. She remembered turkey sandwich rising in her stomach until it reached her chest, burning against her breast.

Her children had followed her into the house. Lauren carried two plastic bags, the ends of her fingers turning red as the handles cut into her hands. Her small bicep muscles were hard under the weight of milk, butter and canned tomatoes. Lauren came in carrying a light bag filled with toilet paper and tissues, swinging it forward and backward, her hair swishing from side to side. Gisella had quickly stuffed the envelope into the back pocket of her skirt. She grabbed the plastic bags from her children's arms and dropped them on the floor. She told them to stop dawdling, to get their school uniforms on; they were running late for the fête. She heard their shrill voices: one telling her they didn't have to wear uniforms to the fête, the other complaining it was Saturday. Before she knew what was happening she was leaping forward in panic, gripping Lauren's hard upper arm and Trina's soft one in her hands. She propelled them forward until they reeled, stumbling over the bags, spilling the contents onto the slate tiles. They ran upstairs, her screeching after them to hurry and get dressed.

Two bodies disappeared and she stumbled across the strewn groceries. She leant forward, regaining her balance, and quickly stuffed the items back in their plastic shells. She removed the envelope from her pocket and smoothed it out on the surface of the table. She picked it back up and turned it over in her hands, pressed it against her face, pulled back the edge of the flap, and pressed it back down again. She held it up to the light, smelled it, held it upright on the tabletop until it fluttered out of her hands and lay flat once more. Finally she picked it up by the corner and took it upstairs to her bedroom. She cracked open the door, looked at the rectangular imprint on the floral doona cover, saw Christian's fob watch was missing from the side table closest to the window. Noticed the few things of his that had indicated the feminine room was shared with a man were also gone.

'Mum! Please, no other kids will have their uniforms on. Can't we wear our tracksuits? Please!'

Lauren's blue eye peeked through the open gap, a strand of blonde hair the only part of her body physically inside the room. Gisella turned abruptly, Lauren jolting as she took the movement as further anger from her mother. Gisella knew none of the other children would be wearing uniforms to the school fête, but in her haste to hide the envelope from them, to veil her fear, she had blurted out anything to get them away from her. Now she had said it though, she knew she would have to stick to her instructions. No child respected a parent who reneged on what they had said.

'Go and put your uniform on. Now. No more arguments.'

Lauren's pleading face held in the crack of the doorway, one eye clear and pale, the other obstructed from view. Gisella turned away.

'Now!'

Gisella kept her face turned toward the window, the lace curtain skewing the view of the neighbour's backyard. She heard Lauren shuffle back to her room, defeated. She walked over to the side table opposite the window, opened the third drawer and placed the envelope beneath her nightdresses.

And that's where it had stayed. Hidden. When she had been moved to the care unit she had made sure the envelope came with her. Gisella hid the envelope inside a folded nightgown, and Lauren packed it neatly into her suitcase, along with her other personals. At the hospital, she watched with held breath as her daughter unpacked the nightclothes, placing them in the narrow drawer of the dresser beside her hospital bed. It had gone unseen and that night, once she was alone, she opened the drawer, unrolled her nightgown and retrieved the envelope from its hiding place. She took it out most nights, as she had in her own home, and turned it over in her hands. She turned it over, held it up to the light, pressed it to her face. Only now her movements weren't as smooth and graceful; they were slow, disjointed. Yet it gave her that same sense of comfort, as though he was still there to speak to her—if she ever decided to listen.

She lay on her bed, holding the envelope tightly, until her fingers began to cramp. She gradually released the paper until it lay against the open palm of her hand. She hung on to the envelope as she hung onto the past. She'd been in the palliative care unit much longer than she'd imagined and she'd opened that drawer more times than she'd thought she would.

She'd spent years imagining the message contained in the envelope, as she did recollecting the day she first saw the houseboat. Christian hadn't told her where they were going that day. His surprises were like that. She guessed he thought he was being exciting, enigmatic. Maybe that's what he had been all along—an enigma. Perhaps that's why she hung on to the tangibility of the Lakes and continued going even after he left. Somehow she believed she would find him, someone she could hold on to. Like his letter. The longer it remained unopened the more tangible his unread words seemed to her.

'Well, what do you think?' he had said.

What did she think of what? The ridiculous over-sized red ribbon tied all the way around the houseboat or the preposterousness of the situation?

'It's… it's… is it yours?'

'No, silly,' he said.

'Mine?' she hesitated.

'Ours. Ours Sunshine.'

'But why? How?'

He had taken her loss of words for excitement. He had lifted her up and carried her over the threshold, wobbling on the gangway until she thought he'd drop her in the cold water. He took her tighter hold on him as a sign of affection. He placed her down gently on the decking but didn't let go.

'What do you say? Our honeymoon vessel? I'd like to carry you over the threshold in a white gown with lace trimming,' he looked her up and down and blushed, 'and lace, you know.'

She punched him playfully. 'You're not serious?'

'I am. Never been surer. I can picture us. You. Me. A couple of kids. They'll grow up on these Lakes. The place where we first fell in love.'

'We can't afford…'

'Don't you go getting practical on me woman. I love you. I want to marry you and take care of you,' and that blush again, 'and have babies with you. What do you say?'

'I, ah, I…'

'I'll take it as a yes then. I thought we could marry in the summer. That way we've got the whole season out here. I've got leave owing. We could take a month. More even.'

And that's how it had happened. Without her ever saying 'yes' they had married. They had christened the houseboat more times than she could remember and her whole life had been spread out beautifully before her. She was pregnant by the following summer. Then everything started to change. The morning sickness that had her retching over the side of the boat marked the beginning of her life being taken over by something bigger than herself, and it scared her.

Soon the houseboat stopped being charming and started being a chore. She couldn't sit at the table when she was pregnant with the girls because her stomach was too large. When the girls were born she constantly worried they would fall overboard and be taken by the Lakes.

'It's not safe. They could slip under the railing so easily,' she implored Christian.

'You're a good mother Gisella. I know they'll be fine with you to worry about them all the time.'

'It's not a holiday. I spend the whole time watching where they are.'

'Don't you love it here anymore?'

'Of course I do. But it's not practical. And it's expensive.'

'Don't I take care of you good enough?'

'Yes, yes. You have a great job Christian. You're a wonderful provider. It's just, maybe we should think about… Never mind,' she trailed off, 'I'll fix dinner.'

The quarrels they had over the cost of running the houseboat continued. They became one of many arguments about money, children, houses, jobs, cleaning, shopping, when all she really wanted to tell him was that she was so desperately unhappy. She wanted the honeymoon back. She wanted the 'her' that had somehow disappeared with marriage and children. Instead, she felt herself slipping away. She became angry at Christian. She blamed him for the freedom he had that he took for granted. And then, finally he took that freedom and fled, and she so wanted him back. She kept the houseboat, the part of herself that still linked her to him, even though she couldn't afford it. Not with two kids to raise. She remembered how she thought that by keeping it she was somehow making up for all the complaints she'd made about it, and about him. She imagined he could sense what she'd given up to keep the boat and would come back telling her how sorry he was he'd left. Yet now she lay mounted on pillows staring at the TV screen with the sound turned down, clutching his letter in her hand and holding onto the last legacy of their shattered lives he had left her.

15

Lauren swam out in long, even strokes until she reached the centre of the lake. She stopped to tread water—pedalling her legs and twisting her torso at the same time so she moved slowly around in a circle. It calmed her as she felt the water's resistance and she took in the shoreline. Some parts offered a sandy bank, others nothing but tea-tree rising up from the water to the edge of the horizon. Once she'd come full circle, she stared out at the faraway township, with its matchbox cars and dollhouses scattered among twists of road and clumps of bracken. She began moving backwards. Back to the last time the cool water had managed to relieve the ache in her temples, before there was too much heat in her head for the lake to take away. Then, as if the water itself contained the stories of the past, the memories returned.

When she awoke that last morning in Loch Sport, the hot Northerly was pushing its way into the boat through every gap and crack. She pushed aside the flimsy curtain above her bunk and brilliant sunlight hit her in the face. She blinked, adjusting to the light, and looked out at the water. Small white caps covered the lake, like tiny boats bobbing up and down. Lauren felt her head expanding and she shut the curtain again, but it was too late. She lay back on her bunk and heard echoes of Trina turning on a tap and her mother rustling in her handbag. A door opened.

'We're going into Sale to do some shopping. Are you coming?' her mother asked.

'No thanks,' Lauren whispered.

'Don't think you can laze about all the time. I expect you to put in as much as your sister does. We'll be back by lunch.'

After they had left Lauren lay still, eyes closed tight, until the room became too hot for her to breathe in. She moved outside to the pontoon, lay down, and submerged her whole head in the water, remaining immersed until she couldn't hold her breath any longer. Flicking her long hair back, she allowed the water to drip down her back and over her arms. She sat cross-legged on the deck, the hot breeze drying her hair too quickly. She was about to dive in again when the calmness surrounding her was interrupted by the roar of a speedboat. Materialising on the horizon, it zigzagged towards her, avoiding the crests of the waves, whitewash forming a path behind the boat. From a distance it appeared to be the James' boat, but she knew Mr James wasn't crazy enough to take a speedboat out when the lake was so choppy. As it neared, she realised it was his boat, but she could also see that it wasn't Mr James driving. It was his son, Hal.

By the time Lauren's hair was crisp and dry, Hal had pulled up beside her. The boat idled in the water, filling the air with the smell of petrol. He bobbed up and down with the waves.

'Hi... Lauren?'

'Yeah,' Lauren chuckled, knowing he still sometimes

mixed the two of them up, even though he'd been seeing Trina for weeks.

'Trina about?'

'She's gone into Sale with Mum. They won't be back till lunchtime.'

'Oh, bummer! She was gonna try and get out of it so we could sneak off for a while.'

'Does your dad know you've taken his boat out?'

'Maybe.' Lauren could tell from the gleam in his eye he didn't.

'Should you be out in this wind?' Lauren asked, watching Hal's familiar smile.

'It'll be right. She hasn't let me down yet.'

Lauren attempted a frown, but she never managed to stay serious for too long when she was around Hal.

'Wanna come out for a spin?' he asked.

'I dunno. Mum'll be back soon.'

'Come on, we'll be out half an hour. Tops.'

'Looks a bit choppy.'

'Don't be a bore.'

Lauren was never one to refuse a challenge so she allowed Hal to grasp her by the forearm as she jumped across to the boat.

'You can let go of my arm now.' Lauren said, once safely inside the cabin.

'Yeah, yeah. Ah, let's go.'

Lauren fell back against the seat as Hal shifted the boat into gear. The nose tilted and the horizon disappeared, coming into view again once Hal had it on an even plane.

'Point Wilson?' Hal asked.

'A bit far isn't it?'

'Come on! I packed some sausages so me and Trina could have a barbie. I don't want 'em to go to waste.'

'Okay.'

He smiled and veered toward the point. As it slowed and tilted, Lauren allowed the wind and spray to hit her face. She began to think coming out on the boat with Hal was a bad idea, and her head began to feel hot again. As the boat turned in a sharp arc it dipped on one side and she leant towards the water. The wind tugged at her scalp, trying to drag her into the water as her hair stretched out behind her, like long pieces of kelp. She lent further over the edge of the boat, until her hair was almost touching the water. Hal pulled at the back of her shirt and she whipped her head back, flicking him with her hair.

'What?' she cried.

'Don't do that.'

'Why not?'

'You might fall out.'

'Oh, you're so protective, Prince Charming.'

'Not funny,' Hal said, his voice suddenly serious.

'Geez, I was only joking.'

Lauren sat back and stared out at the rows of tea-tree lining the banks as they flew along the surface of the water. She loved the way the lake seemed to stretch out forever. At each turn there were more hills, covered in thick green foliage. It was exhilarating moving along so quickly, the wind pulling her cheeks back and making her eyes water. She felt a freedom she had longed for since she first set foot on the houseboat. It was so intolerably slow as it meandered its way along the edge of the Lakes. In the speedboat she was actually moving towards something, away from the familiar and into unknown waters.

They made their way around the point in a wide arc, avoiding rocks and the choppier water they created. The boat slowed and began to lift and sink as waves came at them from all directions. Her stomach rose and fell and her body jarred as they hit each wave. She held on more tightly, but still lurched forward and back as the boat's hull lifted and fell, trying to pry her from her seat.

'Should we go back?' Lauren asked.

'It'll be all right. This bit's always rough'

Lauren sat quietly, trying not to appear nervous. She closed her eyes and tried to pre-empt each wave they hit. Eventually, she stopped hearing the strain of the motor and opened her eyes. They rounded the point and Hal headed in towards a sandy piece of shore. The boat decelerated when he switched it into neutral. He steered through the thick seaweed that turned the water black in the shallows and drove onto the sandy shore. They both clambered out, Lauren jumping off the side into knee-deep water. She felt the tickle of seaweed swirling around her shins and pushed it away. Hal tied the boat to a log with a thick length of rope.

'See? Easy!' Hal said, triumphantly.

He grabbed a small blue esky out of the back of the boat and carried it to the barbecue area. Lauren followed.

She sat at the picnic table, the shade from the tea-trees providing little relief from the growing heat. Hal pushed some twigs into a hole beneath the barbecue plate and lit a match to it. A tiny flame erupted and then disappeared just as quickly, leaving a small orange glow. He removed a string of sausages and cut them deftly with a knife, placing them in a haphazard row on the barbecue plate. He pierced each one and fat oozed from the meat. He stepped back as the plate sizzled then moved closer again, repeating the same routine with each sausage. Tiny beads of sweat formed a layer on his forehead.

'Shouldn't be long,' he said, unnecessarily Lauren thought.

'Sorry Trina's not here,' she replied.

'She's told me about your mother. Well, a bit anyway.'

'What's she said about Mum?' Lauren found herself getting defensive, not that she was really sure why. Maybe it was embarrassment, that her mother treated her different than her friends' mothers treated them.

'You know, her rages and stuff? That's what Trina calls them.'

'Rages? I never knew that's how she'd put it.' Hal looked surprised. 'Trina and I don't really talk about it. I s'pose there's no need to. It's just the way things are.'

'Right. I wouldn't be putting up with that shit. You two should stand up to her.'

'That what you think, is it?'

'Yeah, well, no, not really. Can't say I ever do the same with my olds. It's a pecking order thing, hey?'

'Pecking order? I like to think humans are a bit above the level of chickens.'

Then he laughed. She liked it when he laughed. She began to wonder what she was doing there. Why had she come? She shouldn't have. But maybe like her sister, she wanted someone to take her away, even if it was the wrong person. Lauren turned away, and watched a small flock of black swans wading in the shallows where the seaweed was thickest. The birds performed a dance of their own, stretching out their long necks before dipping into the water. A swan's head disappeared for almost a minute before its bright orange beak broke the surface, a slim piece of seaweed dangling around its slender neck. Beads of water glistened on its back as it curved its neck back into a position, making it appear like it was posing for a photograph. Another swan repeated the same action. The repetitive movement was mesmerising as Lauren watched the rehearsal.

'Chow down,' Hal said, placing a cardboard plate topped with charcoal sausages on the table.

'Thanks,' Lauren replied.

He produced a loaf of bread and offered it to Lauren. She took a piece and held it in her palm. She grabbed a sausage by one end and quickly placed it on the bread.

'Sauce?'

'Thanks.'

His hand brushed hers as she took the bottle from him, and she shivered though it was still hot. They ate in silence, waving away the flies that had quickly gathered and trying to slap away a growing swarm of mosquitoes at their legs.

'Forgot to bring the Rid,' Hal said, waving his arm across the diminishing plate of sausages.

Lauren wondered whether his comment was an apology for the insect invasion or an attempt at trying to break the growing uncomfortable silence. She guessed it was the latter but wasn't sure how to change the steps they danced. She knew, just as he did, they were in a place they shouldn't be and now there was no way out.

Lauren quickly finished her last sausage just as the shade lengthened and darkened across the picnic area.

'I think we should head back, I'm being eaten alive.'

'Yeah, sorry I didn't bring the Rid.'

'It's getting late anyway.'

They packed up the esky quickly and Hal carried it back to the boat. He untied the rope from the log and pushed the boat off the coarse sand. Lauren waded into the water, the seaweed swirling faster now around her shins. She lifted her leg onto the side of the boat but struggled to push herself up. Hal smirked as she balanced with one leg outstretched, her elbows resting on the edge of the boat. He hesitated before stepping towards her, reaching his arms out to help pull her up.

'I can do it myself,' Lauren said.

She pushed on her elbows and managed to topple head first onto the vinyl seat. She righted herself hurriedly.

'Very glamorous,' Hal joked, the laughter returning to his eyes.

Lauren punched him playfully on the arm.

'Ahh!' he yelled, feigning injury.

Still pretending she'd hurt him, he hung his arm limply over the side of the boat while turning the key in the ignition with the other. The motor filled the lake with noise. The swans lifted their heavy bodies from the lake's surface, their wings stretching out, a black sheet, before resettling as they landed on the water again. They bobbed with the ripples their own disturbance had made, their necks held in a question mark while they waited for the shallow water to become still once more.

Hal accelerated slowly, turning the wheel so they faced the open lake.

'This arm's no good. You're gonna have to drive us back,' he said, playfully dangling his arm over the edge of the boat.

Lauren laughed.

'I'm serious,' he joked.

'Really? You don't mind if I drive?'

Lauren climbed across to the front while Hal shifted into the passenger seat.

'I've never driven a speedboat before.'

'It's easy. Just push the throttle forward until you've reached about 35 knots then pull it back until the boat's level again.'

Lauren did as he said, watching the horizon disappear as the nose lifted.

'Okay, now pull it back.'

She pulled back on the lever and the familiar line of tea-tree came into view once more.

'Bit faster.'

Her heart rate began to accelerate with the boat. The wind pushed her hair back and her eyes began to water. She felt like the lake was hers as she directed the boat over and between whitecaps dotting the water. Unlike the stifling heat on the houseboat, the dry, hot wind seemed to revitalise her.

'Feels good, don't it?'

Lauren had almost forgotten she wasn't alone on the lake as Hal abruptly brought her back from her sense of timeless-ness. She was heading back to the houseboat. Back to the still, thick air. Back to the cramped rooms with their miniature appliances and furniture. She felt like Alice in Wonderland—she was growing but the house was staying the same size. She was banging her head against the roof, pounding away until it ached. She was trying to stretch her limbs but the walls were closing in on her. And then there was her mother, and Trina, all trying to breathe the same air. She didn't want to go back. She wanted to scream into the wind to lift her and take her across the lake and to the home where she belonged.

'You okay?'

The sun's rays swirled, spiralling towards her.

'I think I need something to drink. Got any water?'

Hal lifted the seats, searching amongst pieces of rope, rags and an old beach towel that was so dry you could almost break it. He pushed aside half a can of WD40 rusted around the rim.

'Lift your butt.'

She moved across, feeling the boat trying to take on its own direction, but stuck on the route Lauren had set. Hal produced a small plastic bottle, half full with bright yellow liquid.

'Here.'

'I'm not drinking that.'

'Don't be such a girl. It's just left over from the other day. Might be a bit flat is all.'

Lauren took the bottle, opened the lid and wiped the rim with the edge of her shirt. The soft drink was hot and flat, but it managed to relieve the feeling that her mouth was filled with sand.

'Shit!' Hal said, his eyes suddenly glued to the rear vision mirror. He pushed Lauren out of the way. Her teeth hit the edge of the bottle, causing warm drink to dribble down her chin and drip onto her chest.

'Thanks.' Lauren brushed away the bright yellow dots that had settled on her top. But she knew Hal wasn't paying any attention to her stained clothing. He sat beside her, the seriousness she had glimpsed at Point Wilson turning his eyes a darker shade of brown.

'Fuck it.'

'What?'

'Look behind you.'

Lauren needn't have turned to see the dark grey sky rapidly being painted over clear blue. At that moment thick drops fell on her head and shoulders and a cool wind replaced the hot breeze instantaneously.

Before questions even formed in her head, Lauren was given the answer. It came in thundering clarity as she felt her legs shift into her torso and her torso rise up to her neck. As the nose of the boat dived over the wave, Lauren's neck crunched against her spine. She stared out through the water-spattered windscreen at the white crests that signalled to her, to them, to turn back.

'Hang on!' Hal yelled as though she were on the other side of the lake.

She saw his darkened eyes and held face, and for the first time felt afraid in his presence. This wasn't like the discomfort she had felt at Point Wilson; this made her stomach churn more than the waves hitting the boat did. She gripped the stained white vinyl edging and closed her eyes against the storm. The boat decelerated as Hal turned it out towards the centre of the lake. The waves hit harder as the boat continued to rise and fall sharply.

Lauren opened her eyes to a darkened sky. Thick black

clouds now covered it entirely, leaving only a dull white glow where the sun tried to force its way through the clouds, as rain and light fought one another.

'Shouldn't we go in, towards the shore?'

'Yeah! Great idea. If you want me to drive her into a sandbar.'

'But…'

Lauren looked into his dark face again. Her vision became misty as her eyes began to sting. She wondered if Hal had ever shown this side of himself to Trina. How had he acted towards her when they were alone together? Was he the joker like he was with her, calling her clumsy? Or would he gently grasp her arm and help her board the boat? Maybe he became serious, just some of the time. But did his eyes ever darken like they had now, making her feel like a jellyfish, unable to move except where the current took it? She couldn't imagine Trina being with anyone who made her eyes water until she had to turn her face away. But then Trina wouldn't be as childish as her. She'd yell back at him and tell him to take her straight to shore, where the waves couldn't smash her insides to bits.

Suddenly the boat began to turn in an arc. Hal's hands were pushing on the wheel as he leaned away from her.

'What are you doing?' she screamed.

'We're gonna have to turn back to the Point.'

'What?'

'It's too rough. We'll have to wait till the storm passes.'

'But I have to be back before Mum and Trina get home.'

'Take a look at the fucking water! We're not gonna make it back in this weather.'

Hal turned the boat in a wide arc until they were heading back towards Point Wilson. And as the boat turned, so did

Lauren's world. She thought she was heading away from the storm towards calmer water, but instead she was coursing into the eye where the shadows were longest and darkest. She would reach out her shadow fingers to the other side of the lake, but as always they wouldn't stretch to the far bank. She wouldn't be able to scramble to safety. She would be held in the darkness.

16

Trina tore at the linoleum lining on the houseboat floor in the soft heat of the second morning. As she struggled to lift one side, Lauren wordlessly joined her at the opposite end. Though difficult at first, by the time they'd loosened up the edges, the rest of the flooring fell away easily. It was satisfying, tearing off large pieces and tossing them aside. Together they reaped the houseboat back to its core, exposing its soft underbelly. The soreness in Trina's hands and the perspiration beading on her forehead was somehow comforting; Lauren too had relaxed under the fervour of work. Soon the floor lay open and smooth beneath their feet, and the deck was piled high with thick pieces of lino. Trina was tempted to tell her sister how freeing it seemed to destroy the place. To rip it back and take out everything that had become stained over the years.

Instead she silently lifted the sheer curtains from the rails. She slid the dust-covered material along the curtain rods, wrapped it in her hands, and tossed it on top of the growing pile on the decking. When Trina reached for the brown curtains in the kitchen, Lauren cried out for her to stop.

'I want to do that one,' she said.

Trina handed her one end of the curtain rod, feeding it along her hands. Lauren ripped at the curtain, tearing it roughly, pulling until the material was freed from the rod, gradually exposing the beige plastic. Trina considered explaining how to do it more easily but when she glanced at her sister's face and saw how it had changed from blank to animated, she changed her mind. She allowed Lauren to remove the last shreds of fabric hanging towards the floor. She wasn't sure whether Lauren had said 'thanks', but even if she hadn't spoken, Trina knew gratitude floated in the air between them at that moment. They lifted the heavy remnants in their tiring arms and threw them over to the decking. Frayed ends dangled from the edges of their mound of rubbish, fanning out on the water's surface. They sat in the pile of debris, relishing the moment.

'What would Mum say about this mess?' Trina joked.

'Nothing, it'd just be a slap across the back of the knees,' Lauren admitted.

'That all? For *this*?' Trina questioned, gesturing at the pile. Her tone was light-hearted though and Lauren knew that was as far as they were willing to go on the topic.

'What have you girls been doing?' Trina heard her husband exclaim. Lauren giggled at Graham's reaction. She sounded the same as she had when they were children, racing for the bus. It was then she realised it was as schoolgirls she had last heard her sister's laugh.

Graham stumbled over the junk, balancing planks of wood in his arms. 'How am I going to build this decking with all that crap lying there?'

'Thanks for offering to clean up,' Lauren said.

Trina's defences rose as her sister and her husband exchanged jokes. Instinctively she raced up to Graham, kissing his dry forehead, resting her wet cheek briefly against his.

'Break time? I've got some cool beers here for anyone who's up for it.'

'Sounds great!' Lauren replied.

'We haven't even finished getting the rest of the stuff out for the new flooring yet,' Trina protested.

'I'm sure it can wait ten minutes,' Graham said.

Trina couldn't argue with that sort of logic. Or, more poignantly, she hated Graham and Lauren siding together against her.

'Okay!'

Seeing them laughing, her husband and her sister, brought everything back. The pain of how Lauren had betrayed her that last summer in Loch Sport lingered. She thought she had managed to contain it, as simply as throwing a bucket of water over a flame, but the embers were still burning. She had just ignored it. The first thing she recalled about that day was the searing temperature. Unlike the hot breeze blowing across the lake, the heat in Sale had been stiflingly still. She had stepped into a captured world, suspended in time, and she was the only one moving. She and her mother shopped under a burning sun, crossing the bitumen roads and concrete alleyways between arcades. The heat wrapped itself around her, squeezing her sides until she felt the life would be sapped out of her. Standing in the shade of the shop fronts failed to relieve her breathlessness. She remembered entering the newsagency. It was as though molecules of heat had trapped themselves in the small space, making Trina dizzy.

A fan whirred, trying to create air; movement where there was none.

Her mother seemed to spend forever in the shop, the strained whirring of the fan filling Trina's ears. The shop-keeper was a small woman, dressed in a light cotton dress, dark blue with tiny white polka dots that swirled faster the longer Trina stared. The woman's smooth skin glistened with dampness, her pink lips held tight as though she was trying to keep the heat from entering her body. Trina couldn't remember why, but she became angry at her mother for staying in the newsagency so long. It was as though they were taking the air this slight woman needed so desperately. She stood in front of the fan, her skirt flaring out, and perused magazines she didn't have any money or interest in buying. She picked up a copy of *Woman's Day*, flicked through the glossy pages, paused on the fashion spread and then returned it to the wooden slats holding the magazines in place. She did the same with *TV Week*, *Cleo* and *Cosmopolitan*. Before long Trina realised she intended to pick up each of them one by one, repeating the same flick, pause, flick, return. It wasn't until she picked up *Dolly*, featuring a slender, long-haired girl no older than Trina on the cover, that she ripped the magazine out of her mother's hands. She was supposed to be off having a barbie with Hal, not stuck in some sauna of a shop, bored stupid. Lauren should be the one here. She had somewhere to go, away from the confines of the houseboat, and from an ever watchful eye.

'You can't just pick them all up and read them,' she snapped.

'I'm not reading, I'm looking. How am I supposed to know which one I want if I don't see what's in them?'

'You're not going to buy any.'

'I might.'

'What with? Monopoly money?'

Her mother's eyes flicked up at the shopkeeper then back at her, widening as they bore into Trina's face. Her voice lowered as her pupils constricted, catlike, into two thin slits.

'Don't you *ever* talk about money in front of anyone *ever* again. *Ever*. You hear me?' she hissed.

The word 'ever', emphasised for effect, was like a cold cloud hitting a hot one, and the thunder roared in her ears. But unlike the many storms she had viewed from the deck across a darkening lake, relief from the heat had not yet arrived with pelting rain and cooling winds. The storm was still manifesting in a cloudless sky and Trina waited anxiously for it to hit. But it would not come until late in the afternoon, when they returned to the houseboat.

Trina's mother grasped her hand, squeezing her fingers until they became numb. Trapped, she tried desperately not to let her slippery, sweaty hand slip from her mother's grip. She felt her arm being pulled from her shoulder as she was dragged out onto the hot asphalt. The rest of the day blurred, like looking through the mirage that hung over the main road of Sale. Distorted. Vague. Impenetrable. She recalled being dragged around the central strip of shops as her mother purchased groceries. Fruit and veggies from the small, dark fresh food store. Scratchy toilet paper and foul-smelling, plain white soap from the discount shop. Day old bread from the bakery. Anything left to buy was obtained from a dingy grocery store. Her mother said it was much cheaper than the fancy supermarket down the road. Who needs aisles lit up with perfectly placed assortments of tantalising foods or to have their bags packed for them?

Trina never understood why her mother insisted on this fortnightly ritual; taking all day to save a couple of dollars. As an adult Trina always shopped weekly, at the largest supermarket chain within a five minute drive.

Finally, after shopping, and a brief stop for a dry ham and cheese sandwich from a tiny café hidden down one of the narrow alleyways, they loaded the groceries into the back of the station wagon and made the long journey home. Despite Trina's pleas, her mother refused to turn on the air-conditioning, claiming it used up too much fuel. Trina knew arguing further that day would be useless. She remembered another feeling – besides thinking she was about to melt into the vinyl seat. Not numbness, or dizziness, but somewhere in between. A little like the dream she sometimes had where she was a puppet in a bizarre life-sized theatre show. Her legs, arms and head were suspended, and someone else, an invisible force, manipulated her movements. She had no control over her body and felt jelly-like, as though her bones had been removed. They were about halfway home when she had this sensation. It only lasted for a few minutes, but she always remembered it. Maybe because it felt so foreign. Maybe it was guilt for standing up Hal. Perhaps anger at her mother for forcing her to go into Sale. Was it jealousy at her sister, who had been able to stay behind? Or was it just from the intensity of the heat? She was never able to find an answer and yet the memory was still vivid.

The jelly-like moment had passed by the time they reached Loch Sport. They were unloading groceries, her mother screaming out for Lauren to help them, when Trina became free of her mother's hold. Lauren was about to take her place. It seemed, where her mother was concerned, either child fitted, and either would do. Usually Trina was relieved to have the attention diverted from her, yet on this particular day there was a churning in the pit of her stomach, like nervousness on the first day at school.

At first it didn't occur to her to wonder herself where Lauren had gone. All she knew was her mother was busy scouring the houseboat as though her sister would miraculously appear from beneath her small bunk and yell 'Surprise!' When Lauren failed to materialise, her mother's focus returned to Trina.

The screen door flew open. 'Do you know where she is?' her mother demanded.

'No!'

'If you know and you're not telling me I'll…'

'I don't know where she is.'

'You two don't pull a stunt like this without filling each other in on the details. You're always putting your heads together when you think I'm not listening. Well I won't stand for it anymore. You tell me where she's gone.'

'I have no idea,' Trina said, helplessly.

Before Trina knew what was happening, she had fallen onto the hard decking, her face burning hot where her mother had hit her. Stunned, she attempted to rise to her feet, but before she had managed to straighten her knees her mother had grasped her by the hair and was pulling her to the edge of the deck. Trina's head was forced between the railings.

'Where could she be? Out on the lake?'

'I don't know,' Trina muttered, staring at the pontoon below.

Her mother pulled her head back and swivelled her around sharply. Pushing her in the back, Trina was propelled along the side decking to the rear of the boat.

'Has she gone into Loch Sport? Or up to Golden Beach? What do you think?'

Trina shrugged.

'Maybe she's gone off with that little boyfriend of hers. Or is he yours?'

Trina hung her head, staring intently on the timber slats beneath her. The words stung more than the slaps.

'You think I don't know what you girls get up to? Maybe you're sharing him. Is that it?'

Trina was shocked by her mother's knowledge of her sneaking off to see Hal. But with it came the revelation that perhaps Lauren really was with Hal.

'She wouldn't be with him.'

'Get out of my sight,' her mother screamed.

Trina jumped across from the houseboat to the sandy shore. She ran up the beach onto the boat landing. She knew searching for Lauren and Hal was useless but, unsure what else to do, she looked anyway. Glancing right and left she crossed the carpark and headed towards the walkway, disappearing into the tea-tree. She made her way along the pebbled path, rolling her ankles repeatedly on the small tree roots that forced their way through the ground. She reached the end of the walkway, where the tea-tree met the shore. She looked along the sandy bank but didn't see anything except for a few piles of seaweed and some scraggly seagulls scavenging for food. She thought about navigating down the steep embankment. She pushed aside the thin prickly branches and peered down but it was too dense with trees and grass for her to descend. She had come to the end of the path and there was nowhere to go but back to the boat. She continued to stare out between the narrow branches at the lake. Abandoning her search she turned back and for the first time noticed dark grey clouds gathering on the horizon. She watched the growing darkness until mosquitoes gathered at her legs. She slapped them roughly, leaving red marks on her calves and thighs.

'I can't even go for a fucking walk around here!' she screamed.

But the insects only mirrored her frustration. From the moment they had arrived at the houseboat she had experienced those niggling stings. Like the mozzie bites she often found covering her legs and arms, and hidden between her toes, there was a constant irritation, an itching that seemed to always stay with her. Hal had managed to take that away. Their time together made her forget her bites for a short while, and she didn't feel as trapped on that houseboat as she knew Lauren did.

Now that was being taken away from her too. By her mother and by Lauren. She wasn't sure Lauren was with Hal but she couldn't think of anywhere else she could be.

Trina slapped at the mozzies landing on her legs and arms as she returned to the boat. She hoped her mother had calmed down. Experience told her she would be more subdued by now, quietly seething in her anger. And that's exactly how Trina found her, sitting in her white cane chair, staring out at the lake as though she could will Lauren to come home. Trina walked along the side walkway and opened the screen door; loud enough so her mother knew she was back, but not too much to focus the attention on herself.

'Couldn't find her,' she said.

Then she went to the small bedroom she shared with Lauren and sat on her bunk. She stared out the tiny window above her. She could see all the way along the side decking to the back of the boat. She saw the right arm of the cane chair and her mother's elbow, pointing out to the side. She glimpsed the lake and from this position watched the storm approach. Heavy drops of rain fell from the opening above. The wind whipped the water into a frenzy. Thin, jagged streaks of lightning lit up the sky, followed by a crackling thunder.

The storm lasted only an hour, but with it came the cool change the town had been holding its breath for and the news the houseboat had been waiting for. It arrived via a white and cobalt blue speedboat. Lauren emerged from the boat and took her place on the deck, while Hal remained behind the protection of the steering wheel. Trina's mother soon appeared at the edge of the railing. Trina made her way gingerly to the screen door. Standing to one side of it, she could walk through if necessary but it was just as easy to hide behind.

Trina felt once more as she had in the car earlier that day. The movements of her body and mind were manipulated again by an invisible force. Where relief and guilt usually came, she instead felt relief and anger. Her alliance sat not with her sibling as it usually did, but shifted to her mother. Not because they were both angry Lauren was late home or because Lauren had taken the freedom Trina had sought through Hal. It was the look in Lauren's eyes when she came home that told her she had betrayed the trust they still had. From that point on her mother began to manipulate Trina like a puppeteer.

'Where the hell were you?' her mother screamed.

'On the boat,' Lauren said.

'Do I have eyes?'

Lauren remained silent.

'Do… I… have… eyes?'

'Yes.'

'Then can I see you've been off in some speeding boat?'

'Yes.'

'Then answer me properly. Where have you been?'

'Point Wilson,' she mumbled.

'What did you say? We can't hear you. Can we Trina?'

Trina stepped forward as she was motioned to the pontoon. She looked at Hal, his face scarlet, his eyes darting everywhere but at her. She looked at her sister and their eyes locked. Pain mirrored pain, but she didn't understand what it represented in Lauren. Trina put it down to fear and guilt. What else could it be? Trina looked down and noticed a small tear in the side of Lauren's floral skirt. The puppeteer pulled her strings again.

'Point Wilson,' Lauren repeated louder but no more confidently than before.

As though Hal had only just appeared, Trina watched her mother shift focus. Her eyes blazed and Hal's began to dart around more furiously.

'I think you ought to leave, don't you?'

Trina wondered why she had bothered to add the 'don't you?' at the end of her sentence. He was clearly not being asked a question. But she knew her mother liked to finish a statement with a question. It emphasised the point more to her victim that they have no choice; that they are powerless to argue. And Hal wasn't one to miss a point. Trina tried to catch his eye, but he wasn't giving anything away. Without focusing his attention on any of them he reversed the boat, swung it around in a tight arc and drove off.

Lauren kept her eyes downcast, her face expressionless.

'What were you doing at Point Wilson with that boy?'

'Waiting.'

'Don't get smart with me. Look at me when I'm talking to you.'

Lauren's eyes lifted to meet her mother's. Trina was not sure what she expected, but she expected something. Anger or fear. Something. But Lauren's eyes were lifeless and unseeing. She stared forward and blankly listened to her mother talking, yelling, screaming. When it was all over and Lauren was sent inside she moved slowly, as though she were the puppet, not Trina.

She didn't know what to make of Lauren's reaction. Did she feel that badly she had frozen to the spot? Was she that afraid of her mother, or of her? The strength of her response only confirmed the worst for Trina. If Lauren had been innocent in all this she would have waved her arms about, telling them they were wrong and explaining how she'd just gone for a spin in the boat and the storm had come up so they had to wait it out. Trina knew Lauren well enough to expect her to tell her story, no matter what the consequences were and no matter what accusations her mother threw at her. She hadn't. She had just stood there, unable even to look them in the eyes.

Trina felt her anger rise and gather momentum. She'd been mad at Lauren before, or distant on occasion, but this was something else entirely and she was afraid.

'I have to get out of here.'

'Don't go. I know you're hurting. I think we should talk about it.'

Unlike her mother had hoped, Trina did not feel bonded to her in a shared pain. She did not go running into her arms. She did not rest her head on her chest and wet it with tears. She ran for the second time that day, into the tea-tree, as though its spiked branches could offer her comfort as they screamed against the wind.

17

'Beer? Hello, anyone in there?'

'Ah, thanks Hon,' Trina said, taking a stubby.

'So, do you think you'll get a decent price for it?' Graham asked, cracking open his beer.

'Right now? I wouldn't pay a cent,' Lauren joked.

'But can you picture it? With the new lino down, and curtains, and paint?'

'It'll probably cost us more than we'll get,' Trina said.

'God, after what we're going through, we'd better get something for it,' Lauren said.

'Yeah, well, it'll be done soon and we can go our separate ways again. Don't worry about that,' Trina snapped.

'That's not what I meant. This has been much harder than I imagined. And truth be known I am glad you guys are here. There's no way I would have been able to do it on my own.'

'Yeah, it's a shit of a job and quite frankly, I don't care whether we do get anything for it or not. I hate this bloody boat.'

'Don't we all?'

'Except Mum.'

'I think she hated it most of all.'

'Yeah, then why were we here every summer?'

Lauren shrugged, but Trina knew she was right. Their mother *had* hated it most of all.

18

Gisella sat in a semi-upright position, her body tucked into the sheets tightly as though to prevent her from escaping. She knew the end was near now. Trina and Lauren would be sorting out their differences, putting the past in a solid box where it belonged. Locked tightly and ready to gather dust in an upstairs attic. Hidden. Lost. Forgotten. She knew she had made the right decision when she ordered the boat to be set back down on the Lakes that last time. She was not going to put the houseboat on the Lakes for the summer season only to have it lie empty yet again. This was it. This time it would have a purpose—and an ending.

Gisella reached over to the side table. She pulled on the small ceramic knob until the drawer opened far enough for her to reach in. She felt beneath the satins and cottons that made up her nightgowns. Between materials she felt thin paper, and completed her nightly routine of withdrawing the envelope. The ritual of holding it between her careworn fingers, of turning it slowly, smelling the mixed scent of musk and grain, and pressing it to her chest. She held it to the light then brought it back in close to her body, imagining the words that were formed in neat cursive handwriting.

She had replayed the letter in her mind so many times over the years she knew them by rote. It began with an intro-duction—and then an apology.

My dearest Gisella,

I am so sorry to be writing you this letter. Life with you and the girls has been truly magical. Maybe that was the trouble. It was too special to be real. But now I have awoken and reality has taken over. The truth is I have a past that I tried to ignore. I tried to dream it out of existence but it has returned. For the safety of you and the girls I cannot reveal any details. It is best if you remain ignorant. What I must tell you is that it is necessary for me to leave, for I cannot put my family's life in jeopardy. I hope one day I can return, and that we can be reu-nited as a family, but right now I must disappear. Take care of yourself and the children. I dream of the day we can sail away on the houseboat together, all four of us.

Love Always,
Christian.

She had taken those words into her heart. She had repeated those lines a thousand times. She had pictured him walking back through her front door with his open-mouthed smile that forced his eyes shut. He would be holding a worn suit-case but would wear a brand new navy blue suit and starched white shirt. His tie would be made of red silk, but would sit slightly askew. His arms would be filled with gifts. Jewellery for her and expensive lingerie. He'd carry teddy bears for the girls—because in his eyes they would still only be six years old. He'd drop the gifts to the floor when he saw her.

They would pause for a moment, his arms empty, her hand gripping the dining chair for support. Then simultaneously they would rush towards each other and embrace, holding one another still, feeling each other tremble. Tears would fill her eyes—and his. As they moved to kiss, Lauren and Trina would race through the door, recognise their father immediately despite the years that had passed, and all four of them would clutch one other—never to let go again.

After a while, they would slowly pull apart. Christian would take each of them in and likewise his family would look at him. He would look different—older, more knowing, softer. At the same time they would know he was exactly the same. They would realise they had lost nothing. Only time. And time could be made up. He would get down on his knees to talk to the children at eye level. But by now their eyes would be above his as he slowly realised they'd grown. He would glance up at them and ask them, quite seriously, if they'd been looking after the houseboat for him. They'd nod their heads vigorously and Gisella would smile. Just smile and tell him it had been waiting for him all along.

But eventually her imaginings changed. That horrible last summer when the heat was at its hottest and the air was at its stillest her future was taken away. Foolishly she'd believed she was in control. She had gone without, had forced her children to go without in order to keep the houseboat. She'd sold her car and lived off rice and pasta until she thought she'd vomit if she had to eat it one more time. She'd bought clothes from the opportunity shop, despite her embarrassment and disgust at wearing something that was second-hand. She'd cancelled pay TV and magazine subscriptions. She went for ten dollar haircuts and didn't have her tooth capped. All to keep the houseboat. To keep a part of Christian with her.

Maybe she would have had to lose a few of those luxuries anyway. After all, most of the income went with Christian. But she wouldn't have lost all of it. Not if she'd sold the houseboat when he first left. Every year she told herself it would be the last vacation to Loch Sport. It would be the last time she'd pay out money to keep it on the water. But it was his dream to live on the houseboat one day. To meander up and down the lake in a peaceful existence. To hang a line over the edge and cook fresh snapper over a hot grill and converse with the locals and watch the swans float over seaweed. She couldn't let go of his dream, for one day he would return and she would offer it to him like God giving Moses the Ten Commandments. The answers.

That summer changed everything. She knew she could never go back there. She knew what they'd be saying about her children and about her. But still she couldn't bring herself to sell it. She couldn't sell her hope. Without hope there was nothing. And so it had sat there, rotting away, and she hadn't done anything but let it simmer, gathering moss and filling itself with dust and cobwebs and God knows what else. It was falling apart, and for what? Another Christmas had passed and nothing had changed. She could still see Lauren's face that last day spent at Loch Sport, and it still brought a tear to her eye.

Gisella had exhausted all her energy, had let her anger out after Lauren returned with that Hal boy standing there as though nothing had happened. She stood motionless, staring at her daughter, waiting for the excuses to come. But Lauren only stared back at her. Her responses were usually so simple and automatic. If she was angry at her children she would yell at them and they would yell back. They would scream at each other, not listening, just screaming back and forth until Gisella's voice rose higher than her children's and they backed down. Then the tears would come, from both sides. The children would repent and she would accept, delivering their punishment like a priest giving them penance for confessing their sins. They would slink away, accepting their lot, and all would be as normal again.

But on the day of the storm there was no screaming from Lauren. Gisella had given her the worst of her fury but it just hit a wall, rebounding back at her, intensifying until her voice was little more than a high-pitched squeal. No words, just noise. Still Lauren just stood there. Gisella didn't know where to go next. Had she had a victory? It didn't feel like it. It felt more as though she had lost to an invisible opposition, more powerful because it was just that.

She had tried to regain her position by gathering team members. But Trina had left her to deal with this on her own. She wasn't stupid; she knew Lauren and Trina usually played on the same tag-team. One would disappear or remain quiet while the other engaged in battle. And then they would whisper to each other while she watched television when it was all over. But she had thought Trina would swap teams this time. After all, weren't they on the same side now that Lauren had betrayed them both? Maybe she just needed time, but Gisella needed her at that moment. She needed to witness Trina's accusing eye, her disappointed hunch of the shoulders, so she could gather the strength to continue.

Eventually, it seemed Lauren had decided the game was over too. She sidled past Gisella and entered the cabin. Moments later Gisella heard the click of the bathroom door as it locked behind her. She paced the deck, her anger boiling inside, as though she expected Lauren to emerge any moment, ready for battle at last. The door remained firmly closed. In town her skin had been clammy, her cotton shirt sticking to her body against the humidity of the overcast sky. Now with the change she was cold. Goosebumps covered her limbs. She wrapped her arms around her body, rubbing her hands up and down her arms but still she shivered. She started pacing faster and leant slightly forward over the decking, trying to bring the water closer to her. Staring into the murky water brought no relief, she could not see beyond the surface.

Not knowing what else to do, Gisella headed into the cabin. She knocked on the bathroom door, not softly but not forcefully either. Inquiringly, she thought. There was no response. She knocked a little more loudly than before and heard a shuffling from behind the thin door but there was still no answer.

'Lauren?'

Nothing.

'Lauren?'

Still nothing.

'LAUREN?'

Gisella thought she heard a sniffle, but maybe she had just imagined it.

'We need to talk about what happened today,' Gisella said through the door. 'You can't just ignore it and pretend nothing happened. We're going to talk about this whether you like it or not. I don't know what you were thinking running off like that. It wasn't fair on me and it wasn't fair on your sister. And, it wasn't fair on that boy. You're old enough to realise there's not just you in this world and that means there are consequences for not considering everyone you affect when you make such foolish decisions. So what do you have to say for yourself?'

Instead of a verbal response, Gisella heard the turn of the faucets. She heard the water as it ran from the narrow shower nozzle. This defiance was more than she could bear. She began beating on the door, screaming at Lauren to open up. She had never felt so lacking in control. Her fists hit the door, leaving dark red marks on the side of her hands. They began to ache but still she continued to pelt on the door. She would be answered, and now that she had decided so she seemed unable to stop. She wrenched at the doorknob as though it were not locked, just stuck fast, turning it left and then right, left and then right, faster and faster, screaming, 'Let me in!' Her desperation was growing and she started kicking at the door, lifting her leg high and hitting her foot against it. Finally she felt her body falling forward as the door was pulled from its hinges.

It took her a moment to realise what had happened; she hadn't thought as far as actually knocking the door down. She breathed in deeply, her face burning hot from exertion and frustration. An image of Lauren's defiant face as she reached casually for a towel to cover her nakedness formed in her mind. She would force her to speak. She'd had enough of this foolish silence. But Lauren's face was not defiant and she did not reach across to take a towel from the rail. She stood under the shower, fully clothed, her head hanging as water poured over her shoulders. A thin rivulet of colour trickled down the inside of her legs and a pool of rust coloured water covered the edges of her toes. Gisella gasped involuntarily, covering her mouth with her reddened hand. Lauren slowly lifted her head and looked at her mother. Gisella stood silent, staring at her daughter, the girl she had given birth to. She tried to speak, but there were no words to say. They just looked at each other, Lauren's eyes pleading like they did when she was sick as a child. She bent her elbows, lifting her arms toward Gisella, and whether it was meant as an invitation or not she stepped into the shower with Lauren, the rusty water swirling over both of their toes. She wrapped her arms around her daughter and they both stood shaking under the cold water, gripping each other tightly until the skin on their fingers and toes softened and shrivelled.

19

They all worked solidly on renovating the houseboat over the next two days. Although a lot was done, to Lauren it seemed as though they had achieved nothing. The houseboat was torn back to a skeleton and recreated with a new set of organs, stronger muscles and an unscarred layer of skin. Yet she felt ill every time she returned to the houseboat after a walk or a swim. The air was suffocatingly still even when a breeze was blowing. She couldn't breathe as she tossed and turned on the narrow bunk at night. She was pleased that they were about to take it for a run up to Paynesville. Perhaps the movement would free some of the dust that seemed to clog her every pore.

Earlier that morning Graham had finished installing the new bilge pump. He said with everything mechanical now fixed it had to be run in for eight hours. That meant they'd be taking the boat up to Paynesville and would moor it there for the night.

Lauren had been amazed at how the small expenses added up. Paint, materials, timber, nails. And then there were the unexpected things. Mould discovered under the floor coverings. Two cracked windows. Not only was the cost greater than expected but the time spent there had suddenly extended. First it was another half a day, then another day, and then another two days, until she began to think it would never be finished and she would never get out of there. She noticed Trina's anxiety grow too as she began to talk incessantly of work deadlines missed and frantically tapped away at her laptop in the dusk hours. Her seeming frustration at the lack of mobile reception and inability to send emails came across as something deeper to Lauren.

And what of herself? She was a blank. She felt as though she were the houseboat stripped back but somehow had not kept up with the renovations because she didn't feel restored or complete. She felt nothing, and her focus had remained on tasks and adding up expenses. Just as the houseboat sat still in the water, she was frozen, locked tight. Maybe that was why she was so eager for the houseboat to be taken out on the water. She hoped it would dislodge whatever part of her had managed to become stuck. The plan was for Trina and her to paint the houseboat while Graham finished tinkering with the mechanics. It seemed practical at the time, but she was certain he was still trying to play 'sibling matchmaker'.

Trina and Lauren laid out plastic sheets over the new lino. It hadn't been until after they'd finished gluing the new flooring down that they realised it would have been more practical to do the painting first.

'I've got two rollers here. One pole. You wanna take on the ceilings or the walls?' Trina asked.

Lauren took a roller. 'You're taller than me. You take the ceilings.'

'Are you serious?'

'If you don't want to I don't mind doing it.'

'No, I'll do the ceilings. I don't care. I meant, are you serious about me being taller than you?'

'You are,' Lauren said.

The next thing she knew Trina had disappeared. Lauren took a screwdriver and wedged open the tin of paint. She stirred the thick mix until reddish brown swirls began to colour the white liquid. More swirls of colour appeared until they began to blend in with the white and the paint became pale beige. She poured some into the paint tray, careful not to let too much of the weight of the tin come forward and overfill it. Trina returned with Graham.

'Okay, back to back Lauren.'

'Huh?'

'Back to back. Graham can let us know if one of us is taller.'

Lauren smiled. *This is ridiculous.*

'We don't need to stand back to back. You're taller than me. You were born first. You were bigger than me from the start. One twin always takes a bit more in the womb than the other. You weighed 300 grams more than me. It's on our birth certificates.'

'I did not take more in the womb. Graham, come see.' Trina pressed her back up against Lauren. 'Well, is one of us taller, Hon?'

Lauren felt the tips of Graham's fingers brush her hair lightly. 'You're taller than Lauren.'

'That can't be right,' Trina said.

'What does it matter?' Lauren asked. But Trina just ignored her. She'd forgotten how ruthlessly stubborn she had always been. She always had to be right about everything. And if not, she'd somehow prove how she was.

'It's my shoes. Mine are raised. Lauren's are flat. Take off your shoes.'

'This is stupid. I'm not taking off my shoes.'

'Take them off.'

'Jesus. Can you just take them off Lauren? I wanna get this houseboat moving sometime today,' Graham interjected.

Lauren laughed and took off her shoes.

Graham stepped in close again. 'You're definitely taller, Trina.'

'No, check again!' Trina screamed exasperated.

'It's by less than a centimetre. Hardly noticeable.'

'But not by Lauren. How did she always know this and I didn't?'

'I don't think it really matters, does it?'

'You probably just forgot,' Lauren added. 'I've mixed the paint. Want me to fill your tray?'

'I'll do it,' Trina grumbled.

'Okay, call me up if you need any other differences pointed out,' Graham laughed and disappeared.

Lauren couldn't help smiling. When she first found out Trina had married she'd wondered how anyone could actually choose to live with her sister. But she could see how Graham just let her be and didn't take it on. She wished she could have done that with her sister. With her mother too, for that matter. Maybe then she would have had the guts to put her in care sooner.

It took them until late in the afternoon for the painting to be done. As soon as it was finished Trina raced off to let

Graham know. They were both as keen as each other to get moving. Lauren sat on the front deck waiting for them to get going too and finally, as though answering her call, she heard the whir of the motor as Graham started the boat. It always seemed as though the boat lifted itself up out of the water slightly when it was set in motion, like a weight had been removed. Soon Graham and Trina had joined her on the deck. Graham was covered in a light film of dust from working on the boat. Trina was freshly showered after painting and wore a pure white cotton shirt and beige three quarter length pants. She grasped a bottle of champagne in one hand and held three glasses by their fine stems in the other.

'I thought we should christen the new boat,' she said, 'but I hate to see a perfectly good bottle of bubbly go to waste'.

She set the glasses down on the plastic coated table and expertly opened the bottle. Lauren's heart leapt at the sound of the pop as her sister sent the cork flying over the balcony until it settled on the water like a duck. Trina filled the glasses until they almost frothed over the rim. As the bubbles settled she topped them up before handing them out. She gave the first to Lauren, the second to Graham and the last she held in her uplifted hand.

'To getting the bloody thing up and running,' she said, holding her glass into the middle of the circle they had formed.

Despite herself, Lauren entered the circle too. The sound of their glasses clinking together was somehow spell breaking. The light-headedness she felt after drinking half her glass of champagne was not so much from the effect of the alcohol as a strange sort of relief from the tension that had enveloped them all over the past few days. The three of them quickly polished off three bottles within the space of an hour. The champagne was light and refreshing after all their hard work. It was like the cool breeze that sometimes managed to lift off the icy white caps of the Tasman Sea and blow across to the Lakes. Twilight turned the Lakes flat, and a pleasant silence descended as the houseboat meandered its way across to Paynesville. For the first time Lauren began to feel things had shifted. A week ago she would never have been able to touch glasses with Trina, let alone reside in the same small space with her for any length of time. The shift had been gradual and slow and she only just came to realise that things had changed. Like growth and age it crept up on her without her realising, until something made her understand she was no longer the scared teenager she had once been.

Though Trina appeared a more seasoned drinker to her, it was she who stumbled off to bed before the last bottle of champagne had been opened.

'Nothing like some champers to get her off that laptop,' Graham joked, but Lauren wondered if there was something more to his jibe.

'She's always like that then?'

'Yeah,' Graham laughed.

'I thought it was just because of, you know, missing out on work time to be here. Actually, to be honest, I thought it was more to do with avoidance.'

'Avoidance?'

'Of me.'

'No, I can assure you it's nothing personal. She's practically married to her work.'

'Practically?'

'I tend to get in the way of that a bit.'

Graham popped open the last bottle and filled her glass.

'What about family? Kids? You gonna have any?'

'I want to.'

'Trina doesn't?'

'She says she does.'

'But you don't believe that?'

'There's always one more project to do. One more client to settle with.' Graham took another sip of wine and she knew he was letting on more than he otherwise might have. 'I don't think it's gonna happen.'

'Can't say I blame her.'

'Because your Mum was such a bitch?'

'Trina said that?'

'Calls her that all the time. Not to her face, of course. I don't get it. Your parents are still your parents. My childhood wasn't exactly all fun and frivolity either.'

'I understand her decision.'

'But you stuck around.'

'No, I mean about her not wanting to have kids.'

'Why? You don't want kids either? I thought all women wanted babies.'

Lauren laughed. 'No, I don't know. Maybe. If I met the right person.'

'Why haven't you?'

'That's a bit personal.'

'Sorry.'

'It's okay. I've just been so busy looking after Mum, I haven't really got 'me' time sorted out. Maybe, after she's gone.'

Graham stared at her. Lauren blushed, and finished off her wine. 'Oh God, that sounds so awful, doesn't it?'

'No, me and Trina… we should have helped out more.'

'Not really. We made our own choices about Mum a long time ago.'

'You sound like a forgiving person.'

'Not always.'

'So, what are you girls going to do about selling the boat?' Graham said.

Lauren suspected it was more to fill the silence that had suddenly become awkward, than an expression of real interest.

'I guess we'll put out an ad in the local papers. And in the shop windows maybe. That's generally how things work around here.'

'Behind the times,' Graham scoffed.

'By word of mouth,' Lauren argued.

'Won't it be a bit difficult? I mean, seeing we all live up in the city.'

'They still know how to use a phone, you know,' Lauren said, becoming angered by his attitude.

'I just meant in terms of people inspecting it. You don't expect someone to buy it just from the ad do you?'

'Well, I guess we haven't thought that far ahead. But I'm sure you've got ideas. Why don't you suggest how we sell it? I mean seeing you know all about the people who live around here and about what it's like holidaying on a houseboat.'

Lauren wasn't usually so abrupt. In fact she was completely the opposite. Always accommodating and polite. Nothing was ever too much trouble. But the past few days had somehow pushed her. That combined with a few glasses of wine made her more assertive and she had to admit she liked the feeling.

'I didn't mean to offend you. I just think it's something you and Trina need to think about. Now that it's almost ready.'

'Like I said, an ad in the paper. A few signs. That's all we need. It's not like it's that urgent we sell it.'

'Just as well. I mean, you two may not be aware of this because you've always come here but Loch Sport doesn't get the crowds in. There's not much to see here.'

Lauren's head began to swim. She felt the champagne rising from her stomach and entering her head. It began to ache, the skin stretching tightly across her forehead.

'It's not the summer period yet. Another month and the Lakes will be teeming with boats. It's really good timing, getting it fixed up just before peak tourist season.'

Lauren knew her words were false as she heard them escaping into the suddenly stifling air. Loch Sport was one of the ghost towns along the Gippsland Lakes. Compared to the thriving coastal tourist towns of Lakes Entrance and Metung, Loch Sport was a little known place surrounded by swampland and stretches of kangaroo and emu plains. Houses sold for less than it cost to build them. For sale signs stood in empty blocks of mosquito infested sandy soil until they rotted away. Phone numbers had long since faded away with barely a number recognisable. No one came to the town and no one left it. The one motel remained virtually empty in mid January. Shops closed down until all that was left was a general store and bakery. It was unknown to anyone except those who were born there or those who were looking for somewhere completely secluded. Those who used the Lakes for boating up this end were fisherman and the odd skier who wanted to get away from the crowded atmosphere at Lakes Entrance. She hated to admit it but selling the houseboat was going to be difficult. The combination of alcohol and Graham's questioning made her begin to feel angry towards her mother for the first time since she was a teenager.

'Why the hell *did* our mother bring us here? There's nothing here. There's no one. No wonder Trina and I were so fucking bored when we were kids.'

Lauren's speech slurred as she spoke drunken words through tears. More than anything she felt stupid. Stupid for thinking they had been spoilt, going to Loch Sport each summer. Stupid for feeling guilty for hating it when their mother took them away every year, even though she had little money. Stupid for believing her mother when she told them how much she had sacrificed so her children could enjoy their vacations.

'This place is the arse end of the earth. It's a hole. I hate it. I hate it!'

Before Graham could reply, Lauren mounted the railing and dove into the cold water. She suddenly realised how drunk she was as she struggled in full clothing to paddle away from the houseboat. All she remembered thinking was how she wanted to get away from that boat. To get away from her sister and her too practical husband and swim back to Loch Sport. Not realising it wasn't the place she hated but the things that had happened there. Before she could swim away from her reality she felt Graham's arm across her shoulders. She struggled, refusing to return to the boat. But his arm held firm and she found herself being dragged across the surface of the water. Water entered her nostrils as Graham released her briefly before pulling her back on the deck. She lay in a sodden heap, crying and irrationally babbling about needing to get back in the water and needing to go home. But Graham sat beside her, his arm gripping her elbow. Listening to her sob and babble, and tell him how terrible Loch Sport was and how awful the holidays were. And how she hated this place, and her mother, and Trina. And how she hated her life and looking after her mother and how he was right—Trina and Graham should have shared her burden. But Graham did not fight back, or tell her she was silly, or tell her to shut up, or to have a coffee and a hot shower. He listened. He nodded. He stayed beside her until she had exhausted her words and her tears. Until she finally passed out right there on the deck.

20

Trina drove back along the open stretch of road with the window rolled down, the wind loud against her ears and her hair pushing against her face maniacally. Anger had driven her halfway to Rosedale already, but the feeling was beginning to simmer now and the bare landscape was no longer freeing but morbidly depressing. She no longer felt propelled forward and struggled to continue driving as the view through the windscreen began to blur.

She pulled over, the car tyres screeching in the lightly gravelled dirt at the edges of the highway. She stared out at the flat landscape, covered with thick bunches of bracken. As her eyes adjusted she began to notice emus also shared the space. She wondered if the emus felt frustrated they were unable to take flight. Did they question why they didn't have wings that accommodated for the weight of their large and bulky bodies? Once these irrelevant thoughts drifted from her mind she recalled in clear focus the events of the morning.

She had awoken with the dry horrors and her stomach churning. It took her a moment to become aware of her surroundings. Although she had been staying on the houseboat long enough to wake up knowing where she was, she still felt that slight disorientation upon waking. It was especially pronounced because she awoke to a different environment.

'Oh my God. Graham,' she'd said, shaking his forearm vigorously. 'I fell asleep, where are we?'

'It's okay,' he'd said drowsily. 'Me and Lauren stayed up till the boat had been run in. We anchored it up around midnight—well, I did anyhow.'

To learn they hadn't been drifting aimlessly, running themselves out of fuel and winding up in the centre of an empty lake was such a relief she didn't even think about what Graham had just said until later.

Instead of addressing a crisis that lay beside her, she began on more pressing issues. She wrapped a robe around herself and switched on her mobile phone.

'Bugger, bugger, bugger,' she yelled dramatically. 'Still no bloody reception.'

'Shh, keep your voice down. You'll wake Lauren,' Graham said, attempting to draw her towards him by grasping at the tie on her robe.

'What the fuck does that matter? I need my messages.'

'Don't worry about it. We'll head into Paynesville after breakfast. You'll get coverage there for sure.'

'After breakfast? No, we need to head in straight away. Come on, get up.'

'No, I need some more shut eye. It can wait another couple of hours.'

'What the hell is wrong with you? I was supposed to be back at work today.'

'Yeah, all right. Sorry. I forgot. Just give me a minute.'

'I can't believe you forgot. I can't believe *I* forgot.'

'Give it a rest, will you? Chrissie will handle things for you. Why don't you start looking at what's in front of you for once?'

She couldn't remember the rest of the argument. Maybe because that was all that really needed to be said, that one thing she should have taken notice of. Perhaps if she'd listened properly she would have realised what was going on earlier, and wouldn't now be alone on the side of the road in the middle of nowhere bawling her eyes out like a child. She glanced out at the landscape once more and thought about how she had managed to get herself into this mess.

They had headed into Paynesville just as she'd demanded. As Graham had said, she got clear reception on her mobile there. She rang in to work and was faced with a speech about priorities, and reliability and reviews. Those brief sentences were enough to make Trina go into a panic. She hastily hung up after saying she'd be in the office later that afternoon. Her whole body started burning and her heart beat so rapidly she felt ill. A sharp pain stabbed her in the chest and travelled down her arm.

'I'm having a heart attack!' she screamed, sliding to the ground.

Lauren and Graham rushed over as she struggled to breathe. Graham's face was ashen as he watched her and she felt even more certain from his reaction that it was a heart attack.

'You're just having a panic attack. Sit still. It's okay,' Lauren said softly.

Lauren told her to breathe deeply. In, two, three, four. Out, two, three, four. In, two, three, four. Out, two, three, four. Soon Trina's breathing returned to normal.

'Okay now. One sentence at a time. What's happened?'

Despite Lauren's request, Trina's explanation came out in an explosion of jumbled words and sentences, which ended with her saying she had to get back to work immediately. She would catch a cab back to Loch Sport and get the car and would return the next morning after sorting 'this mess out'. Lauren and Graham seemed remarkably understanding and agreeable—until she realised why they were so keen on the idea.

Trina hurriedly packed a few items into her suitcase while Lauren and Graham sat on the front deck talking about how to sell the houseboat. It seemed they had made headway while sitting up last night. Still, she felt a pang of jealousy that they were working out a plan together—without her. But she didn't have much time to think as her mind drilled over what she could say to explain her situation without sounding like work wasn't her main priority.

'Okay, I'm ready,' she said.

'I'll walk you into the centre of town,' Graham said. He then turned to Lauren. 'Will you be okay for a while?'

Both statements disturbed Trina to an incomprehensible level. On the first Graham had told her he'd walk her in like it was something he'd had to consider. Why would he not at least help her get off safely in a cab? Secondly, what the hell did it mean that he was asking Lauren if she'd be okay?

'What the fuck is going on here?' she blurted.

'Pardon?' Graham said, apparently stunned by the outburst.

'What's all this?' she said pointing ridiculously at Graham and then Lauren repeatedly.

'Lauren's feeling a bit, ah, off colour. You know, after last night. I mean, after having drinks last night'.

'After last night, hey? What exactly did happen last night?'

Graham and Lauren exchanged glances, as though they could telepathically tell each other what they should say. That's when the realisation came.

Trina had stormed off to the sound of Graham yelling after her. She'd heard his footsteps following after her when he was met with no response. But she didn't turn around. She quickened her step and then slipped behind a clump of tea-tree like a child playing hide-and-seek until the footsteps stopped and then began again in the opposite direction.

And now here she was, alone and miserable. As usual she had run away rather than dealing with anything head on. She was so angry at Graham. At Lauren. But most of all at herself. She always took the easy way out. She never dealt with her mother; she left her. She never dealt with her sister hurting her; instead she stopped speaking to Lauren. She didn't deal with the pressures at work; she had resigned from her previous job under the pretence of finding something more challenging. And she didn't deal with her husband betraying her. She gave him the silent treatment. Even when she had resolved not to allow anyone—including her own husband—to get too close, she was still able to get hurt. She still found herself having to bail out.

Well not this time. She turned on the engine and watched the emus scatter away from the road in fright. She indicated out onto the highway and headed back into Loch Sport.

21

Lauren saw that stormy afternoon in one light only. She replayed the events in her mind without variation: images of the rain pelting down and of her and Hal sitting on the picnic table that had burned their skin only hours earlier. Against the ice-cold drops that hit her skin, the warmth beneath her was somehow comforting. As long as she could feel some heat she could imagine an end to the storm. But gradually, as her clothing began to stick to her cold body, the warmth disappeared from beneath her. She rubbed her hand on the timber beside her, then shifted across to the place where her hand had been. The warmth she'd created from rubbing her hands on the bench only lasted a couple of seconds but it was enough to hang on to her hope. She continued this ritual, moving first to the left toward Hal, and then to the right away from him.

'What the hell are you doing?' he asked.

'It's cold.'

'Jump up and down or something then. That's giving me the shits.'

The disturbance in her routine made the warmth disappear before she had heated up her next spot with her hands. She felt her hope disappearing and began to sob.

'What now?' Hal said.

'It's cold,' was all she could say.

'Come here then.'

Lauren nuzzled across toward him and leant her body against his. Cold against hot. Thunder roared in the distance.

'I'm sorry,' she said.

'It's not your fault.'

Though Hal said the words casually, Lauren could feel his heart racing as she leaned against him. It reminded her of a magpie she had found on the side of the road. It was the first time she had walked around the small township of Loch Sport, during the first week of the summer holidays. A red 4WD had raced past her, flicking up dust in the distance. Despite crying out, the vehicle had clipped the magpie, its half flight too slow. She had raced over to the bird, which now lay in the middle of the road. At first she had thought it was dead, but as she came nearer she realised it was still alive. Its wing was bent slightly but otherwise it seemed okay. The magpie wouldn't move from its position though and its eyes had a startled look. She knew it had been stunned. Softly, she had placed the palm of her hand on its small body and felt its heart beating wildly as she desperately tried to move it to the embankment, where it would be safe. But as she tried to coerce the bird, its fast beating heart suddenly stopped. It died of fright. She often wondered if it was the shock of having been hit by the car that killed it, or from fear of her placing her hand upon its chest.

The same kind of fear in now appeared in Hal's eyes. Lauren edged away from him, uncertain, his fear being so closely linked to her own.

'It's going to be okay,' she said.

'Dad's gonna kill me,' Hal said, his voice catching in his throat.

'The storm will pass soon. He probably won't even know you've been gone.'

'Like your mother?'

He brought forward the worry she was holding in. She tried to beat it back, like a water hose turned on a grass fire, but it was useless. The flames were already engulfing her, engulfing him. She fought the fire, fighting images of her mother's screams, her mother's hot hand against her face. She tried to get Hal to do the same before it overcame them both. But he had said the words aloud and it had already become real to him. She continued to walk toward the fire, continued to pretend everything would be okay.

'Look, it's even stopped raining. We'll be able to head back any minute.'

Hal turned his head towards her and Lauren felt a sickening pull on her heart as she looked into his vacant eyes. Her 'What if?' mind told her that if she had just admitted things weren't okay he wouldn't have seen her as the enemy. Where she thought she had lessened the blow, she had only intensified it. Hal turned on her, igniting everything in his path.

'What is it with you? You think saying shit like that's gonna make things any better? We're screwed. You know it. I know it. So stop dicking me around.'

'I'm sorry. I just, I don't think it'll be that bad, really. And anyway there's no point worrying about it. It won't make things any better.' She still couldn't turn back.

'Is that one of your mother's lines?'

'No.'

'It sounds like one of hers. You know you sound more and more like her every day? I thought you were on my side, but you're just like the rest of them, aren't you?'

'What are you talking about? I thought we were friends.'

'How can you sit there like nothing's the fucking matter? It just makes me so mad to see you just sitting there like that. Just yell, or thump your fist on the table, or at least fucking move.'

Hal's heavy hands gripped her shoulders, shaking her so hard her head flopped forward and back involuntarily, like a soft toy.

'Hal!'

Lauren wished she'd been able to scream, but all that came out was a pleading yelp and his fury only seemed to escalate. She tried not to be upset, to be angry, but her lip began to tremble and she became only more timid in the face of the flame.

'What're we gonna do, goddammit? How am I gonna explain this to Dad?'

Lauren searched her mind for answers, for the right response, but she couldn't find it. Hal's voice echoed out on to the lake, telling her how useless she was, worthless, pathetic, as she remained frozen in silence. Suddenly he was reaching for her shirt, grasping at the clinging material like a toddler grabbing on to his mother's skirt to stop from falling.

'What are you doing?' Lauren screamed, shuffling along the bench, small splinters sticking into the back of her thighs.

'Come on. I wanna see you be angry for once.'

'What the hell's gotten into you?'

'You've got it so easy, haven't you? Got Trina to protect you from everything so you don't have to worry about a thing. Well she's not here now.'

'Stop it!'

Lauren turned her back to him, covering her ears like a child blocking out the taunts of the older children in the schoolyard.

No matter how she replayed the next moment, she could never picture exactly how it had happened. She tried to stand outside herself, like she had on that day, and watch the scene from afar in her mind. She could feel herself falling, as though she were diving from the top of a skyscraper. She heard the rip of fabric as her skirt caught on a splinter of timber. She could feel her head hit the edge of the bench. She saw the glare of the re-emerging sun hide his face from view. And then she was someone else, watching her body being twisted and violated.

She had turned her face away then. The lake was dotted with white and yellow flecks. A flock of swans emerged, materialising out of the mist. They bobbed up and down, their black necks held in their customary question marks. Questioning ugliness against their beauty. And then a sound rang out across the lake. It was the sound of her own cry, only she didn't know it at the time. Their question was answered. Their long necks reached out, wings flapped loudly and their heavy bodies lifted from the water. Lauren watched the swans' orange feet drag against the force of the water, until they were lifted, their necks perfectly horizontal as they flew away. She noticed the pure whiteness beneath their wings as they beat them against the wind. Black. White. Black White.

Up. Down. Up. Down. They skimmed the surface of the lake, black dots landing on the opposite side of the lake, where the water was still. Lauren wanted to follow them. She stretched out her shadow fingers, trying to reach the other side of the lake. But her fingers only reached halfway.

When her attention eventually returned to Hal, he was pulling her to her feet. She remembered watching him pull up her knickers. She stood still, like a child being dressed by a parent. He brushed her skirt back down over her legs, though she was too numb to feel it. He reached forward to redo the buttons on her shirt, as though trying to make her look as she had before the change he had just made in her. She somehow managed to avoid his hand, and he groped the empty air. He pulled his arm back slowly as Lauren tightly crossed her shirt over her chest, like a baby wrapped in swaddling. She stood by the picnic table, her arms hanging limply by her sides, as he untied the rope from the boat.

'You coming? Should be calm enough to head back now.'

Lauren tried to comprehend the words but they were all muddled in her head. She could see his lips moving but the sounds didn't seem to make any sense. His tone was casual, the Hal she had always known, as though nothing had happened.

'Come on!' he said, waving her towards him.

Lauren felt her feet walking towards the shoreline. One. Two. One. Two. She walked into the water, alongside the boat, until a rush of water brought back the feeling in her hands, her legs, her toes. She lifted her leg and pulled herself over the side. This time there was no hand to steady her as she landed on the vinyl. She laid there, her head resting on the side of the boat as she headed home. She stared at the tendrils of tea-tree reaching out, lengthening as they rounded the point, reaching the opposite shore. But it was too late. They hadn't stretched out far enough when she needed them to. She hadn't made it across to the other side.

22

It was long after dusk had settled its dark body over the lake that Trina made her way back along the narrow path that afternoon. She headed towards the light shining like a beacon from the houseboat. Part of her wished the light had been turned out so she could sneak back into the houseboat, lie on the bunk opposite Lauren and do nothing more than watch the rise and fall of her chest beneath a thin white sheet as she slept. She wished the only light to guide her was the moon's, its silvery glow reflecting off the lake. The same glow that lit her way on the nights she had snuck home after visiting Hal.

Though she knew she couldn't avoid Lauren forever, she wasn't ready to talk to her yet. At the time she thought it was going to be just like any other argument, but it wasn't until much later that she realised the feeling wasn't going to go away. When she entered the small lounge she found her mother sitting under her reading lamp, its green plastic dome hanging over her head like a halo. Her hands busily clacked together two steel prongs, turning thin yarn into a bulky garment. Trina hated those winter jumpers her mother knitted. She hated the bright, itchy wool with fuzzy designs of puppies or flowers she was forced to wear while all the other girls wore windcheaters in pastel colours. But at that moment her mother's methodical clacking of the needles was somehow reassuring. Trina's movements felt slow, laboured, and the air brighter and thicker, but everything still moved on at the same pace. There was still Vegemite on toast and a glass of orange juice in the morning. There was still the familiar cry of black swans, feeding on seaweed. There was still the clack-clack of her mother's knitting needles. The ritual of her mother's knitting betrayed her into thinking life could continue as usual.

'Where's Lauren?' Trina asked.

'In bed.'

'Sleeping?'

'I don't know. I don't think so.'

Her mother placed her knitting on the table. 'Sit with me for a minute.' She patted the seat beside her. Trina squeezed in beside her mother, smelling the faint aroma of musk on her cardigan.

'I know you're angry.'

'That's an understatement,' Trina said.

'I don't think you should blame Lauren for what happened.'

'How can I not? She stole my boyfr…'

Trina stopped mid-sentence. Though her mother knew she'd been seeing him, and had told her so only hours earlier, her response was automatic.

'Let's not play that little game anymore shall we? It does seem rather pointless now, don't you think?'

Trina felt her face redden, and quickly dropped her head, hiding her face behind her hair. Her mother reached over and tucked it behind her ear, as she was still sometimes compelled to do, and tilted Trina's chin up towards her.

'I want you to listen to me. Lauren's feeling extremely miserable right now.'

'*She* is? What about me?'

'Keep your voice down. We don't want the whole town hearing about it, do we? Now just do as I say, for once, and listen to what your mother has to say.'

Trina's only choice was to listen. She was used to choice being used as this kind of illusionary facet of her life. Invented as a kind of torture, telling her what options she couldn't have.

'Now obviously Lauren knew what she was getting herself into when she decided to step foot on that boat with what's his name.'

'Hal.'

'Don't interrupt me.'

'Sorry.'

'What on God's earth possessed her to do such a thing is a mystery to me, but she did. You can't change that and I can't change that. What I do know is that she didn't think through her decision. And I think there's an important difference there, don't you?'

'No!'

'Don't be flippant with me young lady. I'm trying to help here, because God knows I don't want to be cooped up on this wretched houseboat with the two of you throwing daggers at each other.'

'Then why don't we go home?'

'What did I just tell you? I know you don't want to have

this conversation but you can't keep avoiding the truth all your life, so we're going to have it. Here and now.'

'I don't want to even think about it.'

Trina hated getting upset in front of her mother; it made her feel weak, pathetic. But her mother saw the beginnings of a tremble on Trina's lip and she took a more gentle tone.

'I know you don't want to dear, but fact is fact and avoidance is no cure. I know what Lauren did was wrong and hurtful, and the two of you may never get over it. But that's why I have to tell you this. When I saw Lauren's face I knew no punishment I could deliver would make her feel any worse about what she did. She's her own worst enemy right now, Trina, and I can tell she's deeply sorry for taking your friend away from you. The three of us only have each other and nothing should ever be allowed to break that bond.'

'But she's the one who broke it. Why are you blaming me for this?'

'I'm not blaming you. I just want things to be right again between you. I know you two don't always get along. Especially now you're teenagers. But that's only natural between siblings. You still have something very special, the two of you. Sometimes you are in your own little worlds and you don't see anyone else. Not even me. I remember when the two of you were toddlers, just learning how to speak. I could barely make out a word you two said, but you knew exactly what each other were saying. Oh, and how you used to chatter away to each other. You still have your own language. Don't let a silly boy get in the way of that.'

Gisella picked up her knitting and placed in a small rose-covered carry bag, then zipped it neatly shut.

'Now, off you go to bed. And just give what I said some thought. Okay?'

'Okay.'

Trina pulled away from her mother. She slid her legs that had stuck to the vinyl covered chair like glue away from the table and headed to the bedroom. She tiptoed in and quietly changed into her nightgown. She saw Lauren lying in the bottom bunk, curled up, facing the wall, hair covering her face, and her breath like a gentle sigh. Trina climbed up to the top bunk, flicked back the scratchy blanket, then the white linen sheet and lay on top of the mattress, covering just her toes with the bed covers.

'What did Mum say to you?' Lauren asked, her voice soft as she spoke to the wall.

'Nothing.'

'I heard her talking to you... Trina?'

'I'm tired.'

'Mum didn't want me to talk to you about today, but...'

'I said I'm tired.'

'Are you still mad at me?'

'What do you think?'

'I didn't mean...'

'I don't want to hear about it.'

'Please don't hate me.'

'Then don't talk to me.'

'Do you hate me?'

'I don't know.'

'I don't want you to hate me.'

'Then don't talk to me right now.'

Trina drifted into sleep, after her thoughts finally stopped swirling through her head. She woke late the next morning to the sound of her mother whistling as she filled the kettle, and to the pop of the toaster as it spat out warm bread. She rolled over and peered down at the lower bunk; Lauren's body lay in the same foetal position, facing the wall, the sheet wrapped around her like a bat folding its wings over itself. Her elbow protruded, breaking the egg-like shape her body formed. Trina resented her restfulness. She should have been unable to sleep. She should have got up with heavy bags under her eyes and frazzled hair from tossing and turning all night. But she hadn't been restless. She hadn't moved from that position all night. The soft curve of her back made her look almost peaceful, undisturbed. Trina threw back her sheet, climbed down the bunk ladder, and stepped into the kitchen. Her mother placed a pile of hardening toast before her, then placed down the condiments, naming them in turn as though Trina was unable to figure them out for herself. 'Vegemite... Peanut butter... Strawberry jam...' with an emphasis on the strawberry.

'I'm not hungry.'

'Eat.'

Trina took a piece of toast and smothered it with butter, the knife making a rasping noise as it scraped across the top. Once she had finished with the Vegemite her mother filled a tray with the condiments, placing the rest of the toast on a plate, and took it in to Lauren. Trina felt the toast stick in her throat as she watched her mother return from the bedroom, a closed-lip smile on her face.

'You're giving her breakfast in bed?'

'Go down the shop and get me some lemonade, would

you? And some aspirin. In capsules. Not the tablets.'

'I'm not getting anything for that bitch.'

Her mother grasped her by the front of her nightie, bringing her face up towards hers.

'Don't you ever let me hear you talking about your sister that way. You hear me?' She released her grip with a push against Trina's chest. 'Now do as I asked.'

Her mother pressed the already written list into her hand and Trina had no choice but to pull on a pair of jeans and a t-shirt, wipe down the seat of her rusted bicycle and head down to the general store.

There was no one at the counter when Trina approached with the lemonade and aspirin. She rang the small brass bell that sat by the register and Hal emerged from the cool room.

'Coming!' he yelled out before noticing it was Trina who had rung the bell. When he saw her he dropped the crate of apples he was carrying and they rolled along the floor. He didn't pick them up but made his way to the counter, dodging the apples as he went.

Trina gritted her teeth and stared at the clock on the back wall as she waited for Hal to run up her groceries on the register.

'Three ninety,' he said.

Trina handed him three dollars.

'Um, that's three. Three ninety.'

'It's all I've got.'

'Oh, uh, don't worry about it then.'

'Why'd you do it?' she asked.

'What?'

'What part of 'why' don't you get?'

'I don't know what happened to me. I'm sorry. I wasn't myself.'

'That's all you've got to say?'

'Is she okay?'

'Is who okay?'

'Lauren.'

'Lauren? You're asking me how *Lauren* is?'

'Sorry, I…You're not going to tell anyone about it are you?'

Trina grabbed the plastic bag and ran out of the store. Instead of taking the winding uphill road back to the lake, she turned right and, taking the back streets of Loch Sport, headed towards the treacherous ocean at the Ninety Mile Beach.

She wound her way through the asphalt roads, the bike squeaking as she turned the pedals. The sound became rhythmical; the click, click resounding in time with her feet and her breath. Her thoughts began to fit into the same rhythm and instead of the uneven push and pull of her mind as it sorted through events, she began to balance it out into an even flow. Soon her thoughts became gentle waves, up, down, up, down, until all she thought of was the smooth pedalling motions. Right foot, left foot, right, left, right, left.

She passed through the township, staring at the gardens that whipped by, some no more than a random scattering of wildflowers amongst patches of sandy soil. Others were carefully tended, with neatly arranged flowerbeds, stone edgings and thick, soft lawn. A few were like a shrine, with stone statues of native animals, old wagon wheels and an Australian flag on a pole. But despite the gardens, the houses appeared all alike to Trina; low to the ground, with their short, unpainted stumps holding them up. Thin fibro or weatherboard freshly painted, or flaking away at the edges. Rectangles with small square windows.

The flat, winding road through the township ended and Trina turned right onto the straight stretch of bitumen leading to the ocean. The breeze off the ocean pushed against the bike, and she wobbled from side to side until she'd gained enough momentum to push through the thick air that filled her mouth and turned it dry. The plastic bag hung from the handlebars, creating extra resistance, forcing her to pedal harder along the narrow road. Halfway across the overpass that linked the town to the ocean she stopped, wrenched the rusted stand down and balanced her bike on the edge of the road. She pulled out the bottle of lemonade and let the sweet, bubbly liquid wet her throat.

The air was still. There was nothing but a vast expanse of swampland whichever way she looked, empty except for a few black swans floating on congealing water. The only dryness was from the road itself, as the swamp water licked its edges, trying to cover it with its slick wetness. In winter the road would be impassable, as the swamp stretched its slimy arms over the tar and cut the ocean off from the town completely. But in summer the road was an open pass, linking lake and sea, softness and ferocity, stillness and movement. Trina put the half empty bottle back in the bag and stood in the silence. As though having waited for everything to become still, the eerie call of the black swans echoed across the swamp. Their cries were high-pitched, mournful sounds as though they were calling to each other for help. Perhaps it was just sound against quiet that made the cries so disturbing, but Trina quickly threw her leg back over the seat of her bicycle and made the rest of the journey to the beach.

Trina left her bike in the thick foliage edging the empty carpark. On foot, she made her way up the steep, sandy embankment that led to Ninety Mile Beach. At the top she stopped and took in the glare of pale yellow sand. She looked out to the ocean's aquamarine water churned with white-wash as the waves crashed heavily against the shore. Thick kelp was lifted in the waves, turning the water black, and then crashed down, swirling blue and white over the black. She raced down the steep sand dune, her feet sinking into the soft sand, filling her runners with heat. She didn't stop at the bottom, she kept running down the beach, onto the hard sand, into the water.

Waves hit her chest like a cold arm, trying to push her back onto the sand. She forced her way in, against the waves, shouting into the wind, whipping the water aside with the backs of her arms. Eventually the waves knocked her down, pushing her under with their powerful weight. Trina resurfaced and another wave came tumbling over her like a wall collapsing. Under the water, a swirl of foam veiled her sight until she didn't know which was up and which was down. Her nose hit the sand, hard, as though she'd hit rock. Pain shot up into her skull, pinpricks scattered through her head. She began to gasp, breathing in water instead of air. The water pushed her forward and back until finally it was gone and she was lying on the bank, the water fluid once more as it covered her feet and legs.

Trina lay still for a moment, her head resting against her arm, rubbing the sand that filled her hair against her scalp.

Her nose burned. Thick red drops fell onto the yellow sand and stained it brown. She wiped her finger beneath her nose and looked at her hand, now covered with blood. She gathered water in her hands and splashed it over her face, tasting the salty mixture of blood and seawater as it ran over her lips.

It was past lunchtime when Trina arrived back at the houseboat. She knew it by the deep rumble in her stomach and the hot sun that beamed directly overhead. She placed the lemonade in the small refrigerator and the aspirin on the bench. Her mother was sitting at the table, looking at the newspaper but not reading it. She didn't say anything to Trina about being late, nor did she say anything about her bloodied nose and wet clothing. She merely thanked her for the groceries and returned to reading the paper. Trina made her way to the bedroom and retrieved a book from the shelf opposite the bunks. Lauren still lay facing the wall, sleeping, a half empty glass of water and cold piece of untouched toast on the floor beside her. Trina went outside and sat on the deck with her book. She stayed there for most of the afternoon, trying to read over the sound of her stomach growling. Despite her body telling her she was hungry, she felt nauseous whenever she considered eating.

They remained that way until nightfall. Trina sitting on the deck, her mother sitting at the table, and her sister lying asleep in her bed. But while Trina and her mother shifted when the air turned cool and the shadows stretched across to their side of the lake, Lauren did not. She stayed in her bed for three days, getting up only to shower or to use the toilet. She nibbled at the food her mother gave her and she sipped at lemonade and water. She didn't speak and she didn't move.

She was like a ghost, devoid of sense or feeling, and it scared Trina more than any real ghost ever could. And with her fear came hatred. Hatred because she couldn't comprehend any of it. Hatred because she couldn't talk to someone who wasn't there and because Lauren's pain managed to override hers. Suddenly Lauren had become the victim in all this. Trina didn't know how it had occurred, only that it had, and that no one acknowledged her pain.

23

Lauren sat on the deck watching the light fading like a torch losing battery power. The clouds had been moving rapidly across the sky for the past hour and now hid the sun, muting its strong glow. There was a slight chill and she wanted to go inside to get her cardigan but felt unable to move. Since Trina had left for Melbourne she had become rooted to the spot, immobile. A strange kind of numbness had taken hold as she tried to fathom why Trina had reacted so strongly and with such ferocity. Graham had busied himself with finishing off tasks on the houseboat but she could see he felt that same odd confusion.

'It's weird the way the lake changes colour,' Graham said matter-of-factly as he joined her on the deck.

'It's a chameleon all right.'

'It's beautiful. Fascinating.'

'You see those shadows on the water?' Lauren asked.

'From the trees?'

'Yes. When I was younger I thought they were fingers, reaching out. I thought they were my hands and that if I willed them to stretch far enough, they'd reach to the other side of the lake. Then I'd be able to grab hold of the bank and pull myself over to the other side. But they never did stretch that far, only ever to the middle.'

'Not enough sunlight.'

'I showed Trina one time but she didn't think they looked like fingers. I think it's because she wasn't reaching out for anything, things always came to her.'

Lauren turned to Graham, looking into his blurred face as her head began to pound.

'It's crazy that you two don't get along. I can see you both want to, but neither of you are reaching out. Someone's gotta make the first move, you know. And this is your perfect opportunity.'

Lauren felt the heat in her temples intensify. She was furious at herself for letting her guard down. She had managed not to for years and here she was being vulnerable to one of the few people she should be most wary of. In an attempt to push the heat out of her skull she turned it towards Graham.

'I'm doing this job for my mother because she asked me to. That's it. I'll do it and then I'll go home and our lives will go on as before. I didn't come here to resolve anything.'

'But you could if you wanted?'

'No, because I grew up and I know my fingers will only stretch halfway, and no one's going to meet them in the middle.'

'Maybe she'll be willing to now.'

'I don't think so. And what's more, I don't think she'd be too thrilled knowing you were chatting to me like this.'

Graham opened and closed his mouth like a sideshow puppet. Lauren waited, staring pointedly out at the lake, knowing he had run out of words. It wasn't long before she heard the houseboat door open and then close again behind her. Then she saw herself reflected in the glass door. The image surprised her at first until she realised it was not of herself but of Trina, standing alongside the boat. It had been a long time since she had seen herself in her sister.

'We need to talk,' Trina said clearly and plainly.

'Okay.'

Lauren followed her sister like a soldier responding to a command. They didn't speak as they walked down to the rough sandy shore.

'I know that I over-reacted.'

Lauren was surprised by the comment. She was expecting further accusations and demands.

'I need to realise Graham isn't Hal. And that, well, we're adults now.'

Lauren listened to the words, and at the same time did not. She listened more to the tone of Trina's voice as she launched into an almost pre-rehearsed speech. Perhaps it was pre-rehearsed and they were words she had spoken into the mirror a thousand times but never thought she'd really say.

'You broke any bond we ever had that day,' Trina began.

'*I* broke it. You're blaming *me*?'

'You chose to go off with my, *my* boyfriend. Why didn't you just say no? Why didn't you tell him to piss off and come back later? You knew I was seeing him, didn't you?'

'Yes, I did. And I admit I was naive, stupid, but what happened wasn't my fault.'

'Why not? You think because you saw him first you had the right to him? I know you were always jealous of me. You still are. But I couldn't help it if I was the one he was interested in. We had a chemistry going on. It might've been a teen one, but we had something, and you took that away from me.'

'I *saved* you that day. It was me who was left shattered. Why do you think I looked after Mum all those years? I was hiding. Hiding from the world, from people. It's easier to be hurt by those you love than by strangers.'

'What? And this is all because you stole my boyfriend? Or are you blaming Hal? You were seduced right? You're unbelievable. How about sorry? That's what you should be saying to me. Sorry you can never trust me again.'

'Stole your boyfriend? Hold on a minute. Do you really remember it that way? Is that what suits you? Or is that what Mum told you?'

In her head she was telling Trina the truth, explaining her own version of events as they knew them to be. She was weeping over what was done to her and marvelling at the terrible lies their mother had told. She was watching Trina's face as it crumbled at the knowledge. She was feeling her sister grasp her hand and stare into her eyes as they both realised they had lost what they had once held most dear—one another. But she couldn't speak. She had never been able to tell anyone, and she felt that same sense of shame now as she had after getting back in the speedboat at Point Wilson. As Trina stood staring at her with accusation and hate in her eyes she felt herself disappearing beneath the sand. It opened around her bare ankles and swallowed her, the coarse, hot granules scratching at her legs as she sunk deeper into the earth. She felt everything close in on her, squeezing her chest until she couldn't breathe, covering her mouth so she couldn't speak, filling her nostrils so she could no longer inhale. And as the top of her head was covered over with the particles, she felt herself separate from her sister—totally and permanently. Shadows of tea-tree stretched their tendrils towards her but she could still not grasp those long fingers because they were not real. The one person who could free her had stopped stretching out her hand too long ago for her to remember what it felt like. Finally she gathered enough strength to call out. To at least begin. But by then it was too late. Her mouth filled with sand. She could not speak, and her sister drifted away.

'We're not teenagers anymore,' Trina continued, as though trying to convince herself rather than Lauren.

'Thank God for that,' Lauren heard herself say.

'I don't want to get into talking about the past with you. It's pointless. But it's more difficult than I thought it would be just trying to co-exist like this together.'

'It sounds like an introduction for doing just that, Trina. And quite frankly I'm not willing to stand here while you vent your pent up anger on me. If you can't finish this job, why don't you just pack your bags and go home now? You always were good at getting out when it got too tough.'

As Lauren spoke her sister's face turned from one of held suspension to release. The fear of what was about to unfold was strong, but instead of stopping her it propelled her along. As she continued her attack she felt each distortion of Trina's face give her strength. As her words spilled out like the floodwaters covering the road to Ninety Mile Beach she discovered this was the only way to cloak the past, to cover the tarmac surface with softness. She was cutting the lake off from the ferocity of the surf, permanently and indestructibly.

'That's what you do isn't it?' she continued. 'You're always the one who's right. And if they tell you otherwise you just cut them off. Just like that.'

She watched her sister try to find words of anger to throw back at her, but she had pushed the sand back into Trina's mouth. As she exhaled the grains travelled along her breath to her sister.

'Just tell me this Trina. Why didn't you say anything to me about me going off with Hal that day? Why didn't you ask me why I did it? Or at least tell me I was a bitch? You just refused to talk to me. I still remember asking you if you hated me. And you couldn't even give me that. I don't pretend to be braver or smarter or prettier than you. In fact, I have always believed the opposite to be true, but I do know that I haven't run from my life. I haven't left people choking in my dust.'

'I guess you think I should be more like you. I should tell Mother that everything she's done to us is okay. What's more, I should pander to her every need and allow her sickness to suck the life right out of me. Hey, then I'd be just like you. That's what you want, isn't it?'

As Trina walked away Lauren managed a few muffled words through the sand.

'No, I wouldn't want anyone to be like me.'

Lauren faced the water once more as she heard the dulled shuffling sounds of Trina inside the houseboat, packing her things. Had she not been so angry she would have laughed. Only Trina could spend half an hour packing up an overnight bag. For a brief moment she allowed herself to believe Trina was spending so long because she didn't really want things to finish up this way, but she covered that thought with the knowledge it was just part of Trina's striving for perfection.

'Guess we'll be leaving then,' Graham said, cutting through the noise of her thoughts.

'Shame that,' Lauren said sarcastically.

Graham chose to ignore it.

'Everything's done. Mechanically that is.'

'Thanks.'

'We'll leave our mobile on in case there's a buyer. I put our number in the ad. Seeing as you don't have a mobile. I hope that's …'

'That's fine.'

'Will you be heading off yourself?'

'In a bit. Just a couple of things I want to finish off.'

'It would have been easier to sell if we'd been here for the weekend.'

'You know Graham, I don't really give a shit right now.'

'You women really are a mystery. Why did you both come out here then?'

'Well, I'd like to be philosophical and say it was for closure. But we're really still just doing what Mum wants us to. She may be ill but she still holds the power.'

'Nothing wrong with wanting to do the right thing by her.'

'If only it was that simple.'

'So that's it then. You two are just gonna call it quits?'

'I'm sure we'll get calls on the boat. Main thing was to fix it up. Then we just wait.'

'I didn't mean the boat.'

'Look Graham. You seem like a nice guy and everything but I really don't want to go there with you.'

'Guess I'm just curious. Seems a shame to lose a sister over a boy.'

'You do like to oversimplify things, don't you?' Lauren said trying to sound light.

'Then why don't you explain it to me?'

'Why don't you get your wife to explain it to you?'

'One of the first things that I loved about your sister was that air of mystery she had about her. It's endearing, but it also drives me crazy. Sometimes I wish I could get into her head.'

'Trina and I may be twins but I can assure you I have no idea what goes through her mind.'

She paused and saw in Graham for the first time that he was afraid.

'Actually, I do know the story you've got. Wicked sister steals boyfriend and shows no remorse. That about cover it?'

'No, well, maybe. Not so harsh as that. She was devastated by it.'

'That's not how it happened.'

'I'm sure you had your reasons, but I think even you would struggle to forgive that too easily. And for someone like Trina, it's impossible.'

'I didn't do anything *with* Hal.'

'You know I can't be impartial if that's what you want?'

'Graham, there was nothing consensual going on that day.'

'You mean…?'

'He raped me.' Lauren started laughing. Her words sounded so foreign, fake almost.

'This is a joke?'

'I'm sorry,' she said through tears of laughter. 'I've just never said it before. To anyone. I thought this was supposed to happen in some group therapy session or something.

Definitely not to my sister's husband.'

They said nothing for several minutes as Lauren wiped away her tears with the back of her hand.

'Shit. Aren't I supposed to feel different? Happy? Sad? Angry? All of the above?'

'What about Trina? I can't believe she'd be angry at you about this.'

'She doesn't know it happened.'

'What?'

'I thought she did. Until now.'

'Are you going to tell her?'

'There's no point.'

'But doesn't this change everything?'

'No. It's too late for that.'

Lauren allowed herself to be the one to walk away this time. She traipsed along the grainy shore of the lake, tired of being the one to reach out. This time she would be unreachable.

24

Graham had explained it to Trina three times and still she could not comprehend what he was saying. Every time she opened her ears sand would fill them, keeping his words from sifting through. She felt ill. She tried folding and refolding her shirt as he spoke but each time a sleeve would dangle too low, or the collar would be bent within the creases, and she would have to start again. In the end she screwed it into a ball and squished it into an empty corner of her bag. Something she never did, not even with the dirties. She zipped her bag closed and handed it to Graham automatically.

'What are you doing?' Graham asked.

'I'm ready to go now.'

'You don't mean that.'

'Don't I?' Trina said, taking the bag out to the car herself.

Graham followed her and she could feel the look of incredulity boring into her back. She still couldn't process the words he had said. All she knew was that she had to leave. She pressed the small green button on the keyring and heard the familiar popping as the boot unlocked. She pushed it open with one hand, hefting her bag in with the other. Graham took hold of the boot lid before she could slam it shut again.

'Did you hear what I just told you?'

'So?'

'So aren't you going to do something about it?'

Trina turned and looked straight into her husband's eyes, imploring him to understand something even she herself couldn't. He always managed to come up with the best solution and she wished the same could be true now.

'What am I going to do? Tell me. What can I do?'

'I don't know Trina. But you can't just leave her here. Not now.'

She hated that he was right. She slammed the boot closed and leaned against its rim, staring back at the houseboat. She tried to think of comforting words she could say to try and mend the past, to stitch it all back together like one of the jumpers her mother knitted her. But all she could think about was her anger and the threads unravelled more quickly than she could re-stitch them. She knew she could not plan the correct words in her head before speaking, like she did with most things. She felt Graham continue to stare at her until she could bear it no longer.

'Okay! Okay, I'm going.'

'I'll be here.'

Trina made her way back along the shoreline, her feet seeming to slip deeper and deeper into the loose sand.

25

Gisella sat at the cramped table for several hours that night, numbed not so much by the cold but by the truth of what had happened. She felt her knees hit the cold underneath of the laminex-coated table. She leaned against the seat, the plastic backing that was attached to the wall massaging her back. She took out her needles and the ball of wool that was attached to the beginnings of a shawl, the umbilical cord joining the unfinished with the finished. She began to knit. Pearl one, knit two, pearl one, knit two. She repeated the instructions over and over to herself as she twisted the yarn around the needles. Pearl one, knit two, pearl one, knit two. Soon her fingers stopped shaking as she knitted. The even repetition of the needles clacking together cleared her head and allowed her think more logically. As simply as she turned the ball of wool into a shawl she turned her thoughts into a plan.

She waited until the two girls had gone to bed. She crept to the back end of the boat, peered through the thin curtain that divided the boat neatly in half, and confirmed that Lauren and Trina were asleep. Trina's body was almost an exact reflection of Lauren's, curled into a foetal position, her face towards the wall, the toes of one foot hanging off the edge of the mattress. She could hear them both breathing. Trina's breath was smooth and even. Lauren's caught briefly each time she breathed in. Though it was summer, the night had turned cool and she gently spread the shawl she had knitted on top of Lauren. She covered Trina's toes with an extra blanket. Satisfied they wouldn't wake, Gisella left the bedroom, retrieved her bag, and quietly locked the house-boat as she left. She walked briskly down an empty street of Loch Sport, a sickening mixture of anger and fear pressing against her chest. The pain was so sharp it felt as though she'd been stabbed; had she not experienced it almost ten years earlier she would have thought she was having a heart attack.

The last time she had that chest pain her children only reached her armpits. She had been waiting for them by the school gate. A dark-haired girl skipped along the path, her perfectly plaited braids tied with glossy red ribbon. Gisella knew her as Jenny, probably a friend of Trina's but she couldn't be sure. Trina and Lauren only spoke to one another about their friendships. Never to her. Gisella only ever picked up the details of their lives by pressing her ear against their bedroom door, or by reading notes they had been sent from friends in class. But they were only snippets and Gisella was never quite able to piece it all together.

Jenny's braids swished from side to side, like two snakes trying to entwine but unable to meet. The girl's large blue eyes grew even larger, her pupils dilating, as she saw her mother. She began racing toward the gate, throwing her arms about her mother's thick waist. Mrs Jenny, as Gisella referred to her in her mind, broke into a wide grin as she picked her up and kissed her forehead before planting her back on the asphalt. Gisella turned away and waited for her children to saunter out of the schoolyard. Every day her children were late out of class. Gisella began tapping her foot impatiently, waiting to see her children's glum faces as they sauntered towards her. She wondered today, as she did on most days, why her children never appeared pleased to see her like Jenny did with her mother. She had done nothing to deserve it. She was always there for her children, attending to their every need and whim.

Fumes from the school bus filled Gisella's nostrils. She was usually piling her children into the car by the time the bus pulled out. She glanced at her watch, her anger growing. She would demand an explanation when they came out. In her mind she rehearsed a speech about respect and consideration of others. Then she heard it. Brakes squealed. Mrs Jenny began to scream. Gisella whipped her head around. There was something caught under the wheel of the bus. Gisella squinted her eyes and saw a red ribbon snaking out from the wheel, like it was trying to escape.

People began to crowd around. There was so much noise. Gisella ran up the path to intercept Lauren and Trina at the top. They were running down the concrete, trying to see what the commotion was about. Gisella kept running herself, until mother and children almost collided. She grasped their thin wrists in her hands, pressing her fingers into their flesh.

'What took you girls so long?' she demanded, pulling them back down the path.

'What happened?' they said in unison.

'It's nothing.'

'But we heard someone screaming.'

'Stop being so melodramatic and hurry up.'

When they got to the car she piled her children in as quickly as possible, throwing their flimsy school bags in with them. Gisella put her key in the ignition and revved up the car. Her hands shook but her voice remained controlled.

'I want you two to clean up your room when we get home.'

'The bus. What…?'

'It's a disgrace, and I don't have time to clean up after you. What took you so long today?'

'Mum…'

'I'm very angry at you girls for being so slow coming out. Now I don't want to hear another word for the rest of the trip home. You hear me?'

'Yes, Mum.'

'I said not another word.'

And not another word was spoken. Not on the trip home. Not as they walked up the rickety wooden stairs to the front door. Not as they sat and ate cheese macaroni. Not until bedtime.

'Off to sleep now. Goodnight Lauren. Goodnight Trina.'

She gave them each a kiss on the forehead as usual. Unlike she usually did, she went to collect them in her arms like a mother duck gathering her ducklings close. The movement was so foreign to the twins that they took it as a motion for them to go quickly and scampered up the hallway to their bedrooms.

That night, as the light faded on the house, Gisella felt the pain in her chest intensify until she had to lean forward to stop herself from screaming out in pain. Gisella sat on the brown suede couch, curled up in a ball and let the tears fall from her eyes onto her chest. For the first time since Christian left her, she realised that her children could leave her too. They may not pack their suitcases and walk out the front door never to return, but they could disappear just the same. God could make a mistake, make the wrong move, and who knew what cause and effect would come as a result? How could He foresee every move? He wouldn't want a small child to be taken away but He couldn't keep an eye on every action and reaction. It just wasn't possible. She was sure that was what had occurred that day. It wasn't planned. Cause and effect.

So she determined that evening that she was the only one responsible for the events of her own life. She would not be left alone and afraid. It was only then that her pain was relieved and, protecting her ducklings, she rounded up her children and kept them suffocatingly close so they could never leave her. So she would never again feel such pain against her breast. From that day on she walked them right up to their classrooms and, in the afternoons, waited for them at the bottom of the concrete stairway. She escorted them to the local milk bar and watched them play netball on Saturday mornings with a raven's eye. She closed them in: herself, her Lauren and her Trina, and that was the way she would make sure it stayed.

Though Gisella had done just that, she had ultimately failed. She had placed her wings over her children's exposed bodies, shadowing them from the pain the world can bring. She had kept her fears at bay by ensuring she was the one in control but still she had not been able to prevent her children from being hurt.

She continued walking along the darkened street towards the centre of the township, waiting for the pain to go away, but it intensified as the street lights grew brighter. She stopped once she reached the third crossroad and turned her head from side to side beneath the orange light. It took her only a moment to remember where Hal James lived with his parents and three older brothers. She took a left turn, inland from the lake, and passed the fibro houses with their flower-filled gardens. Though she could barely make out the tufts of orange, red, yellow and purple in the darkness, she knew the streets so well she could almost see them. She pictured the rich front yards that attempted to compensate for the cheap homes they embraced. She stopped at one of the houses. It was identical to the others except for the not-quite-straight lattice edging the makeshift veranda. She stood behind the carport and watched him.

It was as though Hal had been waiting for her. Waiting for her to deliver his punishment. He was leaning against a narrow tea-tree stump, one hand deep in his pocket, the other holding a cigarette. The pain in her chest throbbed, as though she were breathing in his exhaled smoke.

Gisella glanced around at the pile of wood he'd cut. It lay strewn around the yard. The axe lay across the top, as though claiming ownership to the cut logs. Gisella didn't realise she'd been staring at it until she noticed Hal flick his eyes towards the axe and then straight in her direction. She pulled back against the cold concrete wall of the carport and watched with one eye. In an almost instinctive gesture he stretched out his foot and positioned his runner over the axe handle.

She assessed the scene. Hal appeared to be alone. The only light came from the porch, emitting a dull yellow glow that lit the front of the house and reached across the pathway. The house was unusually quiet without the sound of Hal's brothers running and yelling and ignoring the sound of a more high-pitched woman's voice. *The rest of the family must be out*, she thought. She wasn't sure how long she stood there, watching him chain smoke robotically, as though he were programmed to light up when the last cigarette had shrunk to a small brown stump. All she knew was there was a pile of six or seven butts beside him when he finally moved inside the house. And then she didn't know what to do. Somehow she had imagined it would all come to her when she saw him. The anger at seeing his impish face would well up until it bubbled to the surface and exploded into some mad act of violence. She would avenge her children's hurt. Inflict the pain on him she had seen in Lauren's eyes. But all she felt was sick and weak and immobilised as she clung to the solid mass of concrete she hid behind. She stood like that, clutching the carport's edging until her fingers became numb from her heavy grip. She watched the dull light emanating from the windows of the rectangular house. She listened to scuffling sounds and muted bangs. She saw the windows turn dark and stared at Hal's unlit bedroom window. Finally she heard the James' car rattling along the dirt road towards her. It was only then she pried her fingers from the carport and disappeared back into the darkness.

Unlike the determined whip she'd created on the way to the James' place, Gisella ambled slowly back towards the houseboat. She kicked at invisible stones and tripped on invisible tree roots extending towards the centre of the road. She took the long way, walking along the path edging the lake. She passed the closed pizzeria and general store, smelling the faint aroma of milk turned sour. She walked past the more well-to-do homes of the area, with their extended deckings bearing white plastic chairs that glowed in the moonlight. She stared out at the black lake, a thin shaft of silver colouring its centre. She passed the pub she knew would be empty except for the locals who sat on tall stools and leaned their elbows on the edge of the bar until closing time. Soon they would be gone too, leaving fresh imprints in the bar's vinyl coating.

She reached the last sign of civilisation in the small town. The marina. The centre of activity and festivity. Boats bobbed up and down on the blackened water, reminding her of the rubber ducks she used to float in her children's bath. Some were old and weathered: fish stains telling the boats' tales, rope hanging in thick greasy lengths holding onto a buoy or beacon. Others were clean and unscathed: the whites still white, the duco unstained, ropes lying in neat coils, the covers placed protectively over the open canopies. Most were somewhere in between the new and the old: clean but not impeccable, marked but not scarred.

Then she saw it, hidden behind the masts of yachts and bows of fishing boats. Its sharp nose pointed directly towards her, bobbing up and down softly as small waves rose and fell. It sat against the smaller pier—the almost unnoticeable assembly of wood and pylons that made an inverted L-shape against the main jetty. It was really just a place people could keep their boats on the busy summer days while they waited to take them off the launching pad. On the odd occasion people left them at the pier overnight, if too exhausted or too lazy to worry about it until the morning. But this one hadn't made it out of the bay and she knew it wasn't exhaustion or laziness that kept this boat alone on the pier. She couldn't see the sparkle of newness in the darkness, but she could make out the sleek design and neat row of seats in its centre. She could make out enough of the boat's features to know it belonged to Hal's father. She had her answer. She turned around slowly, headed towards the jetty, walked along its length and stepped across to the small pier until she reached the speedboat. It was not long after staring into the vacant cabin that the pain in her chest finally disappeared.

26

On the last night Trina had slept on the houseboat as a teenager she dreamed they were trying to escape. Her mother had pulled them out of bed, wrapped wet towels around them, and handed them each a huge paddle. Lauren was already at the bow of the boat, pushing a giant-sized oar through thick black water, while she dragged her own along the side decking. Her mother was steering the houseboat, and she could hear the motor straining as it cut through seaweed. Trina was calling out, asking what was going on, but no one could hear her. She continued pushing her paddle through the black ink. Then she turned to see Lauren fall from the edge. She screamed and Trina reached out with her paddle for her sister to grab on to. But it was too late; Lauren was sinking beneath the surface and as Trina watched her sink she realised Lauren wasn't drowning, she was burning. The water bubbled from the heat and she watched helplessly as Lauren's skin melted. Then she noticed a rim of red flame lining the lake, the tea-tree surrounding the banks ablaze. Her mother threw a fire blanket over her.

Then she awoke. Her mother was telling her to get out of bed, that they were leaving. Trina scrambled out of bed, still drowsy from sleep, and helped carry their hurriedly packed bags to the car. She glanced across the lake and in the darkness pinpointed where the pier would be. But the pier was not identifiable by the small white light that usually shone at its end. Instead it was illuminated with a dark orange glow. Flame danced on the surface of the lake, its fingers reaching up towards the sky.

'The pier's on fire,' Trina screamed.

She didn't relate the two incidents at first. Fire and leaving. The words didn't match up. It wasn't until almost a week later that she realised the words did go together, she just hadn't known how. She didn't know it when the police came to the door or when she was sent to clean up her room. She didn't even quite know it when she overheard her mother explaining to the police how they had left early that afternoon. But she finally understood when she heard her mother say how sorry she felt for the family, and that she knew Hal had been in trouble before. She lied to the police that it must be hard on the parents when one of their children is out of control. She heard the words *drugs* and *money* and *disappointment* all blend into one. Her mother said she'd be more than happy to make a statement.

It was on that day Trina realised her mother's lectures on honesty and trust and 'doing what's right' were not a reflection of her own beliefs. They were just some of the ways her mother attempted to keep her and Lauren within the folds of her long skirts so they were entombed, like mummified bodies. She told herself the shock at this realisation was what kept her silent that day. She told herself she hadn't been thinking clearly and there wasn't much she could do anyway.

She twisted it around until she believed that perhaps it was Hal who had set fire to the boat. And even if it wasn't, he deserved it because it would make him pay for the way he'd treated her.

In her heart she believed none of these statements. She knew, in a place she dared not look, that it was from fear of her mother that she remained silent. Like a child not wanting to see the scary part of a film, but watching anyway through splayed fingers, she listened to her mother's words, accepting them as the way things were. It wasn't long after that she found herself drifting out of her mother's life. She floated away from her family and created her new life. She moved out of the darkness slowly, like the sun casting a gradual shadow across the pavement, and found the light. And although the brightness blinded her at times, it was warm, and free, and soon she found her sun. Like Hal had almost done, Graham came along and provided her with solace.

27

Lauren remembered little of the days after the storm. She remembered drifting in and out of sleep. She could see her mother's face, a mixture of worry and anger, peering into hers in the brief moments of half wakefulness. She remembered Trina, her absence. Doubt began to fill her mind like a thick fog, blocking out true images and memory. She knew her mother had told Trina what happened. She had heard the rise and fall of discussion and the echoing sound of her name.

She waited for Trina to come in and sit on the edge of the bunk, placing a warm hand over her cold one, in a shared understanding. She waited to hear soft reassurances from the only person who could offer her comfort. She waited for her sister to come and protect her.

But Trina did not come in to say she was sorry this had happened. Instead, she drifted in as a shadow, reaching out not for Lauren but for a book, a dress, a fresh bar of soap for the shower—never for her. Trina acted as though she wasn't even in the room. Lauren began to feel the whole mess was her fault.

Trina had always been right about everything and so Lauren decided this was no different. She would spend the years growing into adulthood believing she was responsible, fighting against everything and blaming no one but herself. More than the day at Point Wilson, Trina's hatred of her tore at her soul until she felt it was no longer there. It was as though, on those days she lay in bed, she was reframing her existence and Trina was sucking the marrow out of her bones. Finally, when her mother announced they were going home, the new Lauren picked herself up, packed her belongings and left Loch Sport for the last time.

Had she been more aware of life as it filtered past her, she would have noticed Trina's anger. She would have seen the burning eyes and gritted teeth that tried to tell her they had two different versions of the same story. Like different versions of a fairy tale, one story was full of treachery and hatred, the other of fear and sadness. Though the characters and the setting were alike, the plot was so different they each took away a different meaning. And so they acted in opposing ways. Lauren noticed that Trina began staying overnight at her friends' more and more often; her life devoted to a contradictory but somehow workable mix of partying and studying in their final year of school. Meanwhile, Lauren would sit on the couch, her legs crossed beneath her doona, while she watched music videos, singing the words between mouthfuls of cereal. It had become a routine part of her life. Unlike Trina, she had developed an aversion to the loud, uncontrollable nature of parties. She hated the girls in their short skirts and halter neck tops. She hated the boys, leering and gawking, and the cacophony of bong smoke and spilt beer, and her growing agitation as people closed in on her space.

Since coming home from Loch Sport and beginning her

last year at high school, Lauren felt things change around her more quickly than she could handle. To deal with the constant shifts she tried to keep as motionless as possible. She had become passive and withdrawn, all the while not realising it was not the world that had changed around her, but she who had changed within it. She stepped back from conversation and friendship and people's outstretched hands. She stopped talking about things and started listening, until the voices dispersed, bored with the monotonous sound of themselves, and there was no one left to hear. Perhaps that was why when she finished school she stayed with her mother, working part-time in a supermarket, while Trina studied and lived on campus at a university on the other side of the city.

Lauren began to feel alone. Before she had welcomed her newfound solitude and wrapped it about herself to keep her warm; now she just felt cold. Lauren and Trina's separateness, since that last time they left the shore of the Lakes, was as physical as it was emotional. They spoke little, if at all, and Trina returned home on weekends less and less often, preferring the company of a large following of friends and acquaintances she had rapidly acquired since leaving home. So Lauren clung on tighter to her mother, until her mother's world became hers and vice versa.

28

Gisella turned the envelope over for the last time. It was time to open it, read the words and face the truth. She could hear the chatter and muted laughter of the nurses on their afternoon break. She slowly peeled back the dog-eared corner and ripped the backing. She tore it until a neat white triangle glared at her at the edge of the yellowing envelope. With shaking fingers she grasped at the white paper and withdrew it, bringing it into the light. The letter was folded forwards, like a greeting card, and she gently pulled back the flap, revealing the dark blue ink handwriting inside.

Sorry.

She turned the piece of paper over in her hands frantically. She flipped it forward and back as though it would change the number of words that etched the paper.

Sorry.

That was all. Written once at the top of the page. That was what she had waited all these years to hear? Sorry. *Sorry.* She screamed the words to the empty room as though it could somehow change it. She tore the paper into angry pieces, throwing them onto the floor like confetti around her bed. At the edge of tears, she began to laugh. Great stomach-wrenching chuckles that made her wheeze. She laughed until thick honey-laden tears fell onto her heaving chest. She laughed until her cheeks ached and her voice became hoarse until a nurse finally came in to see what the old man next door had been complaining about.

'Sorry!' she told the nurse between breaths. 'That's it. *Sorry*.'

She burst into laughter once more as the nurse tried to calm her down. But nothing was going to stop her. The envelope had been opened and all the laughter that had been withheld for the day Christian would return came pouring out. The nurse called out to a doctor on his rounds as he passed the doorway. Gisella saw him nod, his head like a jack-in-the-box, as her body shook up and down. It made her laugh all the more. Soon the doctor returned and the nurse removed her cold hand from Gisella's back. After managing to keep her still long enough, the nurse inserted the needle the doctor had passed her into Gisella's hip.

29

Lauren stood by the edge of the lake. The warmth of the sun was beginning to dissipate as dusk approached. There was a slight chill in the air, enough to make it a little too cold for swimming. She flicked off her thongs, leaving them partially exposed as sand covered the rubber sole. Trina and Graham had left, and she knew only the lake could fill the emptiness that plagued her as it offered its waters to her in gentle spurts along the shoreline. She took a few steps forward until the water lapped over her toes, gently pushing towards the arch in her foot. The water was icy at first but soon her skin adjusted and she stepped in a little further. Thin strips of algae licked at her ankles as the water level rose with the next shuffle forward. Lauren waded further and further into the water. The salt water now lapped around her knees, the backs of them most sensitive to the cold. A little deeper and she felt the coolness press against her navel, making her shiver slightly. She plunged into the water and pushed herself through those first stings of cold until it became just a tingle and finally a calming flow of coolness over her chest and shoulders. Her t-shirt clung to her as she pushed her arms in a circular motion, her legs beating in and out. The resistance of her clothing was somehow reassuring and she paddled towards the houseboat. She swam around its edges in an even breaststroke until her fingers and toes began to feel numbed by the cold.

30

The door of the houseboat was unlocked. Trina opened the screen door slowly without calling out to her sister. It didn't take her long to realise Lauren wasn't there. It took her even less time to notice a flash of white rolling back and forth on the new linoleum with the movement of the boat. Despite its obvious emptiness she picked up the small plastic container and shook it upside down onto her hand. Nothing. She called out to Lauren, but knowing there would be no reply she was already scouring the houseboat's decks before she'd finished her name.

Lauren wasn't there. She ran back out into the thickening air and onto the foreshore, pacing its edges, looking without knowing where to look. She understood the urgency but her mind blurred over with the possibilities and too many thoughts. She tried to clear her head of sand. *The water.* Trina turned her gaze from the shore to the blackening lake. The water lapped hungrily at her heels as though trying to suck her in too. Shadows of tea-tree began to lengthen as dusk fell, and its black shapes made her heart hold still, thinking she had seen Lauren. She screamed out her sister's name, repeating it as though her voice could somehow will her to appear.

31

Gisella was pleased. Everything would be set right now. Her plan was perfect and she knew everything would be fixed once the houseboat was sold and the two girls had resolved their differences. What could be more fitting? The source of all her troubles would bring her family back together again. She liked the irony and it brought on a smile that made her cracked lips bleed. The salty taste of herself brought her comfort and she closed her eyes, shifting into dream.

When the nurse came to give Gisella her afternoon dose of medication, the first thing she saw were the pieces of white paper scattered on the floor. She rolled the trolley by the side of the bed, stopped to pick up the pieces of paper and tossed them into a wastepaper bin. She half-filled a small plastic cup with water and lined up pills neatly in a row on the silver tray. She routinely took out her stethoscope and shook Gisella's arm lightly.

'Mrs …'

There was no response, just the feel of cold flesh. Experience made her realise quickly that she was gone. She leaned over, pressing the buzzer on the side of the bed.

In the palliative care unit procedures were quick and

simple. It didn't take long before Gisella was declared dead. A message was left on Lauren's message bank to call the hospital immediately. Another was recorded on Trina's mobile. It was never long before a family member called back.

32

Lauren noticed the shadows lengthening at the same time as Trina. She saw the long, spindly fingers gradually narrowing and coming closer as she struggled for breath. She pushed against the water, trying to reach them, but her body was getting too heavy as the lake began to consume her. She tried to grasp onto the thin fingers but they would not be held. They teased her, retracting and lengthening with each stroke of her arm towards them. And then they were all around her, taunting her with their blackness, trying to push her under the surface of the water. The shadows she had always thought could save her were helping the lake drown her. She tried to wrench the fingers away from her but they clawed at her face, her shoulders, until she felt herself sinking. Her mouth filled with the acid stench of salt and algae.

Then Lauren heard the faint cry of a swan. It was calling her name and she tried to head towards the sound. She willed it to lift her out of blackness, to take her upon its wings and carry her across the lake. She would soar above the water, as the swan's wings beat black and white against an orange sky. And then she felt it. She was being pulled out of the water. Her heavy limbs were being pulled free from the lake's grip as she felt them turn to liquid. The air around her was icy and she shivered. Fine feather down brushed against her wet stomach and she lay prone against its softness. And she was lifted high above the black abyss as the swan's question mark turned to a horizontal compass point, headed straight for home.

Acknowledgements

I would firstly like to thank all the teachers and my fellow students at Chisholm Institute of TAFE's Professional Writing and Editing course in Frankston who gave me invaluable feedback, taught me so much about the craft of writing and helped me to find my writer's 'voice' during my time there. Most of all, many thanks for the encouragement along the way as I made my first foray into writing this story in Liam Davison's novel writing class. Thanks also to all my other teachers for the many writing tools I was so generously given along the way.

A special mention to my beautiful friends in my workshopping group on the Mornington Peninsula, without whom I could not have done this, and who inspired and motivated me with each and every meeting. Thanks also to everyone who took the time to read *Unloched* during its various stages of its development (you know who you are). Huge thanks to my husband, Neil, who has always been the first to read everything I've ever written.

Many thanks to Gerda and my dad for providing the inspiration for the setting where the book takes place. My characters would not have been able to live and breathe within the perfect setting for this story without the many years I spent holidaying at Loch Sport.

Thank you to the Victorian Premier's Literary Awards for commending the work in its unpublished form and thus enabling me to maintain my faith in the story.

And last, but by no means least, a huge thank you to Michelle Lovi, my wonderful publisher at Odyssey Books. Thank you for believing in my story and for giving it life.

BIOGRAPHY

Candice Lemon-Scott is an Australian author and writer. She has a Bachelor of Communication / Diploma of Arts (Professional Writing and Editing) and was a Media Manager for a number of years. She is also a Literacy Champion for the Literacy Villages program. She has published two works of fiction for children and has had numerous articles featured in print and online publications. *Unloched* is her first novel for adults.

9 780987 232571